# THE SOUTH FORSAKEN

## RACHEL DRUMMOND

ODYSSEY
BOOKS

Published by Odyssey Books in 2015
ISBN 978-1-922200-40-2



www.odysseybooks.com.au

A Cataloguing-in-Publication entry is available from the National Library of Australia

ISBN: 978-1-922200-40-2 (pbk)
ISBN: 978-1-922200-41-9 (ebook)

To the picturesque and still very much alive
City of Geelong


Thanks to Christy Maf, Torres vs. Zombies, Evolution of the
Apocalypse, Zombease.com and Creepercast.
A huge chunk of my encouragement and inspiration came from you!

# Prologue

Justin was hunched alone at his desk, swamped in his oversized HAZMAT suit. He had spent the better part of the public holiday running tests for the science bigwigs and just wanted to go home to a cold beer. His wife and son would be back that afternoon from visiting his in-laws for Christmas, something that he wasn't too broken up over missing if he was going to be honest with himself. He smiled as he imagined Angela's expression when she saw what he had ready for her, though he knew she would be upset when she realised his medication had been ignored in favour of his work.

He twitched minutely as a familiar, unwelcome voice pushed its intrusive self into his skull, breaching his mind and stealing his thoughts from his head.

He had pressed himself harder than usual, wanting to finish this stage of the experiment early. Half an hour longer and he could leave. Half an hour and he would take the meds he had stored in his workspace. Fighting to pull back control, he twitched violently and looked around quickly. He wasn't sure if he was looking for the other he could feel watching him, or for his co-workers, who still didn't know about the schizophrenia he had fought to hide for most of his life.

He picked up the syringe with the current test substance and readied the rat firmly in his other hand. This would be the last, and then he could close everything up and go home. Another jerk had his hand spasming and he looked down in horror, feeling a cold prickle along the back of his neck.

The syringe swayed slightly where it had imbedded itself into the thick fabric of his HAZMAT suit. He hadn't felt anything on his skin though. Maybe the fabric had stopped it? He was sure he hadn't depressed the plunger; this was nothing to worry about. With shaking hands, he inserted the syringe into the rat and pushed, injecting Substance F into the squealing creature before replacing it in the cage. He quickly signed off on the paperwork and cleaned up thoroughly, not wanting to raise any suspicions from the scientists around him. He ducked into the airtight room leading off from the lab, waiting for the decontamination procedures to finish before he ripped the air hose from his back and tore off his helmet. He panted slightly as the first hints of panic sent icy fingers down his spine. He knew his work was risky, just as he knew that if they found out that he had been exposed to the untested trial drug his freedom would be little more than a beloved memory. He would be separated from his family, denied his basic rights; he knew that his history was one of the reasons behind his assignment to this team. He had seen it happen before: the government-funded research team he worked for was given liberties no moral person would entertain.

The CSIRO had recently started work on a synthesised hormone thought to reduce the symptoms of schizophrenia. Justin's team was responsible for the first phase, which introduced a lab-mutated Bornavirus spliced with a variant of toxoplasmosis into a host to simulate the symptoms of schizophrenia. He glanced down at his gloved hand, desperately hoping that the toxic mix had been kept from his skin.

'Everything okay, J?' The intercom clicked and he nodded his head, trying to portray the calmness he didn't feel.

'Yeah, yeah, everything's fine, mate. Just a long day behind the glass.' He jabbed a finger toward the Plexiglass helmet he had dropped to the floor. A rough chuckle rang through the enclosed room and echoed mockingly through his brain. He fought not to react, as disjointed paranoid thoughts clawed at his mind. He glanced down at his arm, frowning at the line of red scratched across the surface of his skin.

Frantically he ducked into the men's room, sparing only a moment to make sure he was alone before scrubbing at his arm. The near scalding water turned his skin an angry red as he soaped and rinsed, repeating until he couldn't take the heat. He moved to the bench, took out his pills and, throwing three of the little green triangles onto his palm, swallowed them dry.

He barely remembered his walk to the car, the trip home twisting into a haze of moving cars and lights. He stumbled in through his front door, guided only by a distant sense that told him he was home. He grabbed a beer from the fridge, throwing back the first mouthful before he walked blankly to the living room, tossing his coat onto the back of the sofa. He sank into the worn recliner and closed his eyes in exhaustion.

It was growing dark when he woke, the click of the door announcing the arrival of his wife and son.

'Dad?' He could hear his son Chris making his way through the house. Justin scratched his arm absently and stood to greet him.

Angela came in and smiled, holding up a thawed, uncooked box of pizza. 'Did you go through all this trouble for me? I feel so special.' She reached up to kiss him but he shied away, the scratch on his arm still fresh in his mind. She frowned.

'I think I picked something up at work,' he muttered, trying to brush it off.

'Is it serious?' she asked, concerned.

'Nah.' He winced as his voice listed high and he coughed to clear his throat. 'Just need to wait a bit, minimise fluid transfers, the usual precaution. To be sure.' He turned just in time to see Chris place his beer back on the table sheepishly, lips still shiny where he had drunk from his dad's bottle.

'Oops.' He wiped his mouth.

Justin paled and his wife's worried frown deepened at his distress.

'What was it? What are you working with?' She knelt beside her son, resting a hand on his brow but he waved her off. Her worried eyes turned to her husband.

Justin held his hands up in what was meant to be a calming gesture. 'Look, I'm sure it's nothing, I barely got scratched. And this happened earlier today. Nothing's happened to me yet, and if I did pick something up I would have been showing *something* by now.' He pushed all of the confidence he didn't feel into his words, and whether it spoke of his skills as an actor or her unwillingness to accept the worst as a possibility, she let it go. It was not mentioned again that night, although her worried gaze darted between her two boys as they moved around the house.

Sleep kept its distance as Justin lay in bed. He looked over Angela where she slept peacefully, and climbed out carefully from between the sheets, stepping softly over the squeaky floorboard and creeping down the familiar stairs. Reaching the fridge, he liberated another beer and slunk over to the recliner, turning on the TV and flipping through the channels, too wired to rest. A thump pulled his attention to the ceiling; he smiled as he followed muffled footsteps as they dragged sleepily from his son's room to his own. Even as a teenager, Chris liked to know that his parents were nearby.

Justin turned back to the TV, just as an audible scream split the silence. He spun to the stairs, taking them two at a time as he ran to his room. The door was open as he approached and the sight that met him threatened to bring him to his knees: Chris held

Angela tightly to him, face buried in her throat, the sheets were dyed a deep red beneath him.

'Oh God,' Justin choked out. His son looked up at the noise and growled at him; his eyes were coated with a milky film, his mouth dripped with blood and spit as his lips peeled back in a growl. Chris dropped the body and lunged toward Justin, who stumbled backward out of the room, slamming the door as he fled. He ran back downstairs to where the light of the TV still illuminated the house and pulled his mobile phone from his jacket, mashing at the buttons.

'Emergency services, how may I direct your call?'

'He attacked Ange! He's eating her!' His words garbled together in his haste to get them out, and then he dropped the phone in fright as a heavy thump rattled the door above him. The wood splintered under the heavy body throwing itself against it. A terrified scream filled the house and for a moment Justin didn't recognise it as his own. He fled past the heavy front door and slammed it shut to wait for the help he desperately hoped was on its way.

# Chapter One

The world ended on Boxing Day, with blowflies providing a droning soundtrack to the summer heat. People nationwide were still recovering from gorging themselves the day before.

Sarah worked in aged care in Geelong and didn't usually get a chance to work in the acute sector. The overload of patients, however, meant they needed all hands on deck and she found herself called in to work at the public hospital. As to be expected, major holidays meant busy emergency wards, and very little time to assimilate the goings on in one case before being called away to work on something completely different. Sarah had spent most of the afternoon tending to her four patients, and forcing down a coffee whenever she could tear herself away.

She nearly overlooked the memo on the desk in the nurse's station; it might have been a normal warning for a potential viral infection that may be seen in newly-admitted patients, briefly reminding nurses of care instructions and advising use of full precautions. Sarah brushed her lank black hair out of her face and picked up the memo to read it properly. The last alert they had been given for a viral outbreak had been the influenza strain last winter, but something about the tone of the memo insisted she pay attention. She decided to play into her paranoia and ducked out into the fire escape to call Jen, a fellow student nurse she had worked with. They'd kept in contact after Jen was moved to the Royal Melbourne Hospital to complete her final year.

'Jen, hey, how are you? How's work?'

'Nope, not doing it,' Jen replied. Her tinny, brusque tone seemed rude to those who were unaccustomed to her personality.

'Doing what?' Sarah asked innocently.

'Small talk? You don't do small talk. What's up?'

Sarah grinned and looked down at the memo in her hand. 'Has your hospital received a memo on this new outbreak?' she asked, purposefully keeping it vague and playing into the tight suspicion that curled down her spine.

'Actually, yes, we got the alert that there was something happening in Geelong. I'm not sure how far it's spread though. We had one of our regional patients come in this morning, hyper-aggressive, extremely violent behaviour. We had to call a code black on him. I think he came from down your way.' She laughed but it sounded strained. 'You know the weirdest thing, though.' Jen paused. 'I was in ED when he came in and I know they pronounced him brain dead. It must have been really close, especially with the ferocity with which he woke up; he damn near flew off the trolley.'

'He came back to life?' Sarah asked incredulously, her voice strangled. She coughed to try to cover it. Jen snorted.

'No, that's not what I said, he was only *clinically* dead. I know what you're thinking, and you're obsessed. I mean that in the nicest way of course.'

'Of course. I know,' Sarah replied, hoping her voice was projecting the reasoned maturity that she wasn't feeling at the moment.

Sarah ended the call standing quietly in the stairwell, two thoughts warring for attention in her mind. It would be easy to walk back on to the floor and dismiss this as a paranoid geek-out moment, finish her shift and go home to her cats. She opened the door, picked the second option and walked back to the nurses' station. Her shift didn't end for another hour, but playing on the fact that she was called in on a public holiday and had cut her break short, she ducked out early and headed down to the emergency ward via the cafeteria to snag another coffee. It might not be the good stuff, but caffeine is caffeine.

Gulping half of the coffee down and logging into the ward computer, she checked the reports for the morning. It wasn't strictly allowed, but who questions a person wearing scrubs in the hospital? She noted the usual cases that had been admitted: a couple of children brought in with nausea and vomiting; four people involved in a car accident, two of whom were released with minor injuries; and two brought in with suspected substance abuse—one currently sleeping it off, the other displaying very aggressive tendencies. That one had to be restrained after attacking a staff member. A note attached to this last patient's history suggested that his father, who had his own history in the hospital's mental health records, had come in with him. It stated that the father had been ranting about mutated viruses and government conspiracies. The doctor who had admitted the young man had called for security to escort his father away from the other patients, assuming the aggressive paranoia to be a result of his schizophrenia.

Sarah looked around to see if anyone she knew was working and smirked slightly when she spotted Nell, a flighty nurse with the unfortunate tendency to babble—something that Sarah now fully intended to exploit.

'Nell! Are you off? I have coffee.' Sarah waggled the half empty coffee cup in the air. Nell followed the movement eagerly; a nurse's addiction was an easy thing to take advantage of. Sarah handed her the cup and they walked out. Nell removed the lid, looking sceptically at the low level of the coffee.

'Evaporation, it's the heat.' Sarah waved off Nell's disgruntled look at the half-empty cup and sat on the low bricks out the front of the hospital. 'I hear you've been having fun this morning?'

Sarah started casually, throwing out the bait. As anticipated, Nell jumped at it eagerly.

'It's been shocking! Not so much in cases—it's been surprisingly slow there—but that one guy … I'm sure it's a full moon tonight! We had to put him in the isolation unit when he came in.' Nell took a sip of the half-warm coffee. 'We were waiting for whatever he was on to leave his system but it didn't, no matter what we pumped in … *or* out! He was so *violent*! The doctors eventually said not to go near him, so we had to stick to suicide obs through the window. When he still wasn't calming down after an hour, Sue went in with security to try to sedate him and take his obs, and he bit her! I don't know what he's on, but I haven't seen anything that does this before! And his dad wasn't much better; he was talking about *killing* him! *Honestly*! His own son! The paramedics that brought them in said their place looked like a slaughter house.'

'Nell, slow down. What case?' She acted ignorant, not wanting to admit to snooping through patient files.

'The substance abuse!' Nell paused, and lowered her voice. 'He killed his mum. He was on such a high that he ripped her apart! They said he was eating her when they came in and another team had to be called in to help them. It took four of them to get him down!' A disgusted look crept over Nell's face.

'Okay, you said he bit Sue. How is she?'

'Not sure, I think they were working on her when you came in. It was pretty bad though. With the amount of blood she was losing, he must have severed an artery.'

Sarah stood up and walked back inside, driven by a need to see what was happening. Nell followed her closely. Sarah wasn't sure what she was looking for—years of horror movies were beginning to play through her head. She needed to find something to either prove or disprove her suspicions.

She swiped the entrance card-reader and walked in just as

a code blue sounded over the intercom. She hurried forward, following the crowd that rushed to a curtained off area. Sarah sucked in a breath, hoping to laugh at her over-blown paranoia. Stepping through the curtain, Sarah saw the resuscitation team working frantically to revive a body on the table. She heard the doctor call for the defibrillator and watched as they applied the shock. Someone thrust a notepad in her hand, yelling at her to take notes if she was planning on 'just standing there'. On auto-pilot she started to write down everything: the meds given, the shock applied, the patient stats being yelled out … every action got recorded into the little book, including the doctor's final statement.

'Time of death … 1500, 26th December 2013.'

A suffocating silence seemed to fill the partitioned area and she felt her heart slow from its panicked pounding to a rate where she felt she could breathe again. Distantly she heard them discussing Sue's family; someone had called up to the next ward to request nurses who didn't personally know or work with Sue to clear the room and prepare her body for her family. The adrenaline leeched from Sarah's system, leaving her feeling drained. She allowed the nurse in charge to guide her to a chair in the office as the rest of the team filed in after her and dropped similarly into the seats littered around the room for the routine debrief.

The team discussed their actions and the outcomes. Sarah read from the notes when asked, relaying everything leading up to the unfortunate death of the nurse involved. The cynical part of Sarah's brain raised an eyebrow and asked *How dead?*

A chime sounded overhead, and a faceless voice called over the loudspeaker. '*Code black, resuscitation bay two, code black!*'

Sarah felt a wave of heat rush through her body, followed by an icy chill. She stared at the curtain she had stood behind moments before.

With adrenaline still coursing through her body, Sarah could almost forgive herself for not noticing the scream that echoed down the hall. As she registered the new chaos that piled itself into her harried brain, she found her feet leading her toward the curtain that separated the bay from the corridor. Her steps led her past the isolation unit where the steady thumps behind thick glass commanded her attention. Her head turned, almost on its own, to look through the thick observation glass. Her hand drifted up absently, hovering in front of the glass that separated her from a young man, his milky eyes seeming to look past her, not following anything in particular. His mouth hung slightly open, a viscous trail of saliva smearing the glass where he was pressed against it. A vicious snarl rattled through her ears and she snatched her hand back, her survival instinct driving her out the door.

The sudden shock of sunlight and overwhelming heat woke her from her wandering thoughts, and she looked up to find that she had left the hospital and was standing on Bellarine Street, facing the staff car park.

'Where are we going? What do we do?' Nell's small voice startled her out of her reverie.

'We?' Sarah frowned in confusion as Nell stared at her with wide, wretched eyes. Sarah hid a grimace at the added responsibility. 'Just keep quiet,' she huffed, walking brusquely to her car. Her nursing training pleaded with her to return and help, but she ignored it, reasoning that her family needed her more. She pulled out her phone and dialled James, newly married and a recent father to daughter Charlie. Her dark-haired, sarcastic geek of a brother made a striking contrast to his tall, blonde, serious wife, Rebecca. Sarah knew that if anyone would be able to empathise with her fears at the moment, it would be James, with whom she had shared so many laughs during horror movie nights when they were growing up. And if this all turned out to be a stress-induced figment of her imagination, he would at least be able to see the funny side of it.

'James?' she said as the phone was picked up.

'No, sorry, he's with Charlie at the moment.' It was Rebecca's voice. 'Sarah? Are you okay? You sound stressed.'

Sarah choked out a laugh. 'I'm really not okay. Can you put me on speaker and go to James please?' There was a muffled jostling and James's voice came distantly through the phone.

'Sarah? What's up?'

Sarah sighed. Now that she had to voice her suspicions she wasn't sure how to word them.

'Sarah?' James questioned; she'd apparently been quiet too long.

'Can you come to Mum's place?' she asked. 'It sounds stupid in my head … I'd rather say this in person.' She could almost hear the look of bemusement that must have passed between James and Rebecca.

'What's wrong?' he pressed, worry teasing into his voice. 'Are Mum and Dad okay?'

'They're fine,' she assured him. 'But something's going on.' She took a deep breath. Knowing he would need something more than a feeling to go on, told him exactly what had happened so far, and explaining her outlandish suspicions as to the cause. To her relief, her brother and his wife didn't laugh. There was another fumbling sound and James's amused voice sounded clearly in her ear.

'It could be nothing; you might be panicking over rubbish.' He sounded like he would really like nothing more than to go back to his family and laugh off the story recounted by his paranoid sister.

'Yes, it might, and by all means, if that's the case, laugh away. But what if it's not?' Sarah heard James heave a sigh.

'What do you want us to do?'

'Your home is all glass, and your fence wouldn't keep anything out. Grab what you need and go to Mum's. She has that high fence and the extra space in the garage flat if we need it. We can work out what's going on from there.'

Sarah hung up feeling drained. This was a situation she had never expected to find herself in. Gritting her teeth, she moved toward her car and walked straight into a pale, shaking Nell.

*Ahh, right*, she mentally corrected herself, *family and miscellaneous others …*

'Nell, don't you need to go home?' Sarah struggled to keep the stressed edge from her voice, not needing the added frustration.

'Mum's overseas. I don't want to be home on my own,' Nell murmured, her voice low and uncertain. Sarah sucked in a deep breath.

'Come on then.' Sarah gestured impatiently toward the car, her eyes drifting to the small green car and onto the stunted boot that hid the bug-out bag she had worked on and carried around for years. She smiled as she slid into the driver's seat, the beginnings of a plan starting to form in her mind.

# Chapter Two

Sarah pulled in at the petrol station down the road, filling up the tank just in case. A squeal of tyres jerked her attention to the front of the car. The crowded sedan in front of her peeled off and swerved along the road, away from the city.

She fumbled a little as she swiped her card at the counter, eyeing the panicked actions of the motorists as they sped past the petrol pumps. More than one took advantage of the panic to avoid paying.

Nell sat wide-eyed in the passenger seat, a pale spooked look fixed on her face. She hadn't said a word since climbing into the car, her stillness in direct contrast to her usual hyperactivity. Sarah remained silent as she climbed back into the driver's seat and sped down the crowded road toward her parents' house.

Sarah's brakes protested the sharp, jerking stop in front of the high iron bars that separated the house from the street. She left her car parked parallel to the house and almost ran through the tall gates, her father's sporty coupe the only car in the driveway. Remembering Nell, Sarah turned to see a shaky figure climb out of the car, although she was unsure whether the shaking was a result of the situation they'd found themselves in, or of the fact that a normally twenty-minute drive had been compressed into ten. She hauled the gates shut behind Nell, fighting against years of disuse to bring them together. The faint squeak of the aged front door announced her mother's arrival.

'Sarah?' Anica was a short woman with sparse greys starting to pepper her short dark hair. She walked slowly out onto the porch and stood with a quizzical look on her face.

'Mum.' Sarah sighed in relief, wanting to laugh at the normalcy of it all. She wanted to laugh off her hyperactive imagination, drive Nell home, then have a coffee with her Mum and listen to her Dad regale her with another debate on AFL vs NRL, trying to sway her decision to rebel against his years of training by choosing the former. The intermittent screech of tyres along nearby Anakie Road suggested otherwise, and she turned to watch the unusually heavy and dangerously fast traffic pouring up the road, eager to put the city behind them. Giving herself a sharp mental shake, Sarah ran to the converted garage behind the house and grabbed the bike chain from behind the door. She hurried to secure it around the gate, locking the group inside the relatively safe, though hopefully temporary shelter afforded to them. Nell had joined Sarah's mother on the porch by this time and had actually hidden behind the bemused Anica, as though that alone would protect her. Sarah shook her head as she walked up the stairs to join them.

'So …' she began. 'We had a bit of an eventful day at work. Could you put the kettle on, Mum?'

The idea of coffee seemed to spur Anica into action and she quickly moved into hostess mode, herding Sarah and Nell indoors and onto the couch. Within five minutes, they all held a coffee and Nell had a plate of biscuits in front of her, for 'the shock'. Anica had thoroughly berated Sarah for her traumatising driving.

Sarah leaned back into her chair. 'Dad, can you call Georgie please?' she asked, turning to where her father sat in his customary recliner, his solid presence seeming to add some calmness to the room. Alex was the quiet type, a pastor and a counsellor for most of his life. His quiet studiousness seemed to directly contrast with Anica's loud, at times brash personality. Her mother was currently displaying her restlessness through a constant stream of questions, as she tried to understand what was happening. Alex picked up his phone and dialled, putting it on speaker.

The phone rang several times before Georgia answered, and her strained voice spoke volumes about the stress she felt. Georgia lived with her fiancé, both serving in the military, on the Adelaide air force base, and her slightly acerbic personality usually kept this sort of emotion well hidden. The fact that she was now displaying her anxiety so openly suggested to Sarah that whatever was going on was big enough to involve the defence force.

'Thank God you're okay!' Georgia blurted out. 'We're not allowed to call out. They're watching us too closely and I couldn't reach my phone without being obvious. I had to make an excuse to leave the room. I was so scared when I hadn't heard anything from you. Are James and Rebecca okay? Are they with you? Are you all safe?' The questions would have continued but Sarah jumped in when Georgia paused for a much-needed breath.

'Georgie, slow down.' Sarah surprised herself with how calm she sounded. 'I'm here with Mum and Dad. James and Rebecca are on their way here with Charlie.' As if summoned by the statement, a furious horn sounded at the gate. Anica walked over to the window.

'They're here,' she said unnecessarily, and walked toward the door

'I'll get it,' Sarah said quickly. 'I put the bike lock on.'

Anica stared at her blankly. 'Why is the bike lock on?' she asked incredulously. 'The gates are way too heavy to steal.'

Sarah ignored her mother's attempt at humour and walked outside, leaving her parents to talk with their absent daughter.

James and Rebecca had parked outside the gates and were taking Charlie out of her car seat. Sarah could see their frightened expressions and quickly moved to undo the lock.

'Going by the traffic out there, I think I've missed a good "I told you so" opportunity.' James's voice had a forced lightness to it that belied his pale face.

She did a double take as she saw their outfits. Rebecca's wasn't a surprise, dressed as she usually was in a skirt and heels. Sarah could understand that, to a point, there was no proof that this was anything more than a panicked request to visit. Why dress for the end of the world if you're just visiting the in-laws? The sceptical part of Sarah's brain scoffed at that before she turned on her brother.

'Seriously? You're potentially running for what may well be your life in what is hypothetically the zombie apocalypse, and you thought *that* was the shirt to do it in?'

James looked down at his artistically styled blood spattered shirt with 'This is my zombie killing shirt' emblazoned across the front.

'Seemed fitting.' He shrugged.

Sarah cocked an eyebrow, hoping her expression read, *I'm so disappointed in your facetious behaviour*, and that it didn't betray the internal laughter she was trying to quash.

Sarah led the family inside, where Alex was speaking softly over the phone with Georgia, his face drawn. Anica was making coffee in the kitchen, with Nell hovering behind her trying to help, but in reality causing more of a hindrance. Secretly Sarah approved, thinking that Nell's flightiness might give Anica something to focus on. She joined Alex, James and Rebecca in the lounge room, throwing a 'hello' toward the phone to announce her presence to Georgia, hoping to prompt her into giving the cliff notes of the conversation. It seemed to be related to their current situation, if Alex's expression was anything to go by.

Georgia's voice was uncharacteristically serious when it filled the room. 'Hey Sarah, how are you?'

'Oh, you know, recovering from Christmas, the usual,' she shot back, voice oozing sarcasm in response to the inane question.

Georgia snorted inelegantly before filling the silence. 'I gather you know something about what's going on down there?' she asked, taking a steadying breath.

'Not really,' Sarah admitted. Even with what she had seen, she wouldn't commit to the idea until someone else seconded it. *Please God, let me be over-reacting!* she silently pleaded. Perhaps it was just an exacerbated viral disease as the memo had said. Jen might have been wrong; they had been hard-core horror fans for years, they had plans in place for the zombie apocalypse, and they certainly had enough material to whip their overactive imaginations into seeing what wasn't there.

'It's happening,' Georgia stated directly, bludgeoning that feeling of hope to a mushy pulp.

'Bugger. Yeah, I figured.' Sarah closed her eyes.

'I have to go, there should be an emergency broadcast released soon. They held it off as long as they could in case the locals were able to contain it.' Georgia sounded tired. 'We're not supposed to release information to the public outside of the official information. They're worried about the panic it could cause. I told Dad what I know. I'll meet you where we said we'd meet.' She carefully side-stepped around using any names, not wanting to take the chance, as slim as it was, that someone would overhear her. There was silence; no one knew how to end the conversation.

'Stay safe,' Sarah said quietly, leaving the rest unsaid, partly because they weren't overly demonstrative as a family, partly because it felt too much like goodbye.

She shook off her low mood, wanting to know what Alex had been told. The tension in the room was suffocating as everyone sat nursing what remained of their cold coffees.

Alex straightened in his seat, drawing the attention to himself.

'As far as I can tell, there seem to be two stories. The first is the official story that is being given to the hospitals. There is a new strain of an unnamed virus that causes uncontrollable violent actions, and staff need to take precautions. Georgia says the unofficial story is that the viral lab is here in Geelong.' He paused, noticing confusion on all their faces. 'You must have heard about it. It was in the news while they were building it. They built a super lab to conduct research into every serious virus known to man here, right in Geelong.' He went back to the story, not wanting to go too far off the track. 'Apparently, one of the long-term research teams was using the Borna virus to test a new schizophrenia drug, mutating the virus with a few different strains, such as toxoplasmosis, to duplicate the disorder in order to trial their new treatment …' He trailed off, waving a hand vaguely. 'Georgia doesn't have specifics—the whole thing was highly experimental. She only heard that somehow, one of the mutated strains was released. There's a rumour that one of the lab techs was infected, but nobody noticed until it was too late. There is someone the military is looking into as a possible source. One of the lab techs admitted his son into ED, after the boy attacked his mother.'

Sarah nodded, thinking back to what she had seen at the hospital. She frowned. 'Did she say what happened to the lab tech?' she asked.

Alex shook his head. 'The last she heard, he had been restrained due to schizophrenic ideations and manic behaviour. He was threatening to kill his son.'

'So, what now?' Rebecca asked, holding Charlie tightly.

Sarah's mind flashed to the countless hours of zombie movies she had watched, laughing at the hapless victims as they aimlessly flung themselves headfirst into hordes of predators. Suddenly the humour seemed a lot more distant, her half-formed plans seemingly irrelevant when facing the stark reality of it all. Everything she knew about zombies agreed on two things: first, they started overseas, not some small, secondary city in Australia. The second and the more immediately relevant point was that they needed to leave.

Alex numbly reached for the remote control and turned on the television. The blonde anchorwoman looked annoyed as she read from the statement in front of her, glancing up and to the side of the camera every now and then as if looking for confirmation, a hint that this might be a prank. The red chaser streamed across the bottom of the screen warning viewers in Geelong to stay off the roads and remain in their houses where possible, or find their nearest refugee centre if they found themselves away from home, or in the city.

'People are advised to keep phone lines clear. Officials are aware of what is happening and, with call centre staff reduced and the huge influx of calls, they are unable to keep up with the demand. The army is being called in and will be setting up roadblocks throughout regional Victoria in an attempt to contain this infection … Really?' She looked to the side again. 'Tezz, this is ridiculous. Is this a joke?' Someone must have motioned the woman to go on, as she picked up the paper once more, her face tight with frustration. 'I repeat. There is a highly infectious virus that has struck residents in Geelong. Victims are showing extreme rage and violent tendencies. There have been reports of the infected attacking others, and fatalities have been reported, though numbers are not known at this point. Towns around the affected area have been put on alert. Residents outside of Geelong are advised to move to the refugee centres that are being set up. The location of your nearest safe location will be sent via the SMS emergency alert system.' The anchorwoman looked to the side again and a slight, brown-haired woman walked up to her, sliding another paper in front of her. 'Oh my …' The anchorwoman paled visibly now, betraying her fear, although she covered it quickly with a thin veneer of professionalism. 'Ladies and gentlemen, this is not a joke. We will be switching over to the emergency broadcast system shortly. Please remain calm and follow instructions as they are released.' Her eyes drifted down to the paper in front of her. A shaking hand reaching toward the paper was the last image before the feed was cut off.

'Georgie is headed to Kaniva,' Sarah said softly, as everyone looked at her askance. 'It's halfway between here and Adelaide, with a tiny population. We always said we'd make that our meeting spot if anything happened.'

'The alert said to stay put.' Anica looked concerned but Sarah shook her head.

'We can't. I saw what it was in the hospital. If we stay here, we'll die. We could maybe survive a week or so, but not forever. If we stay, we risk being stuck here completely, no way out.' She tried to sound nonchalant. 'Don't worry, we're ready for this.' Sarah wasn't sure if she was trying to convince her parents or herself.

A furious whispering drew her attention to where Rebecca and James sat, huddled together.

'James? What's wrong?' Sarah asked.

It was Rebecca who looked up at her. 'I have to find my family,' she said, her voice quiet but strong.

'Call them.' Sarah handed the phone to her. 'I'm sure the authorities have started quarantine procedures and set up the refugee centres. They might have received the same message we did and may already be safely tucked away somewhere. They wouldn't want you to put yourself in danger if they were all fine.'

Rebecca didn't look comforted by the words, but took the phone and dialled as she left the room for privacy.

Sarah pulled her mobile phone from her pocket, eyes widening at the string of alerts that already covered the home screen.

Her Facebook feed had been flooded with concerned queries as to their safety, and asking what the hell was going on. Several of her American contacts were pressing her for details of the 'zombie outbreak' that had struck down half the continent and closed off the airports completely from the rest of the world. She frowned as she read them, wondering how she could have possibly been excited for the apocalypse she found herself in now.

# Chapter Three

Rebecca walked back to the group visibly shaken. James handed Charlie to Anica and walked over to her, wrapping her in a comforting arm.

'Ben was in the hospital,' she said, referring to her brother, her junior by three years. 'Some sports thing. Mum's in the hospital with him. Laura's at home with Dad. He said Mum managed to phone out once but the line was bad and she was whispering so they didn't get too many details. She said something about tunnels under the hospital.' Rebecca seemed to wilt into her husband's arms, the thought of her family stranded in the damned city proving too much for her. 'I told Dad to go to the Queenscliff fort with her. Apparently the emergency refugee centre is being set up there. Laura still doesn't know what's happening. I couldn't tell her, and Dad seems to be completely blindsided. I have no idea what to say.'

James rested his head against Rebecca's, unsure how to offer comfort.

Sarah stood up, breaking through the tense atmosphere. She walked over to the bookshelf and pulled down the Geelong phonebook, thanking her mother's irrational technophobia that led to a hazardous hoarding of paper-based information. The phones may be working at the moment, but there was no telling how long that would last, and the odds were good that the lines would either be jammed or blocked in the near future. She scanned the map of the city, frowning at the crowded buildings and busy roads between them and the hospital, putting that aside for now.

She opened up the local map and traced the area surrounding them, muttering under her breath as she noted the list of stores and facilities in the area. At some point James had started to read the map as well.

'Oh, we need nappies,' he said absently, the normalcy of the comment contrasting dramatically with the situation and causing every head to turn toward him in disbelief. Even James seemed a little taken aback with the comment but recovered quickly. 'What? But we do,' he defended himself. 'The world may be ending, but shit still happens.'

Alex started chuckling quietly, and this seemed to give Anica permission to release a snort of laughter. The dam of hysteria that had been building up in everyone was suddenly unleashed, manifesting in peals of laughter that seemed to dramatically lighten the mood in the house.

As the group settled, Sarah spun the book she had been perusing around to face everyone and sat back.

'So, what we know is that there has been a possible viral outbreak, centring on Geelong, which seems to be *somewhat* fatal. But it is also causing extreme rage in infected people, prompting them to attack other humans, which then passes the infection on to another host.' She specifically avoided referring to zombies, not wanting her family to see it as little more than a movie plot and losing the sense of urgency they needed to keep them moving.

Sarah turned to Rebecca with an apologetic look. 'We have to assume Laura and your dad are safe. I know you've been to that fort. If they have a refugee camp set up and they're in it, they can hole up there pretty well, and they'll have access to governmental assistance if it's run properly.' Rebecca looked decidedly unhappy with this but conceded the point.

'What about my mum? And Ben? They were at the hospital where you said this all started,' she pointed out. Sarah nodded in agreement.

'It may be where the source of the panic started, but they have armies of professionals and security teams and, if they said something about the tunnels, they may have already been moved out of danger. I'm sure they're okay for now, but we'll try our best to get to them.'

She attempted to reassure Rebecca, but by the look on her face it seemed it wasn't working too well. Sarah shook her head slightly. She wasn't going to be able to impress just how bad an idea a foray into the city was. The only thing she could do was try to assure Rebecca they would go find them, *after* everything was safe and organised here. Every evacuation speech she had been made to endure through work or during the bushfire season said that if you weren't safe, you couldn't save anyone else. This was fine in theory, but she wasn't the one being told that her family was not a priority.

'We need supplies,' Sarah said. 'We have water.' She gestured toward the slabs of bottles in the corner. 'And I know Mum has a large supply of food, both canned and in the freezer, so we should be fine for now. I want to go to the camping store. They'll have a lot of things there that will be useful,' she said, tapping her finger on the page-width advertisement in the phone book. 'From there, we'll come back and figure out how to get into the city to the hospital, and then out to Kaniva.'

'Where the hell is Kaniva? And why are we going there?' Nell finally found her voice. 'We're safe here, aren't we? Isn't that why you brought everyone here?' She threw herself backward into the chair.

'I'm not forcing you to come, but I'm not leaving my sister hanging in the middle of nowhere and we have to keep moving.

We have to get as far from here as we can, preferably somewhere with an ocean, or a very large, very long fence between us and those things.' Sarah threw a look at her parents. 'Please keep in mind that whatever this is, and however big it gets, Geelong is the epicentre. There is no telling how long we can survive here or how long the supplies will hold out.' She fell silent, sinking onto the arm of Alex's chair.

'We'll take cars where we can, but that might be few and far between depending on the condition of the roads. Best prepare for an extended stroll.' She looked at Rebecca's heels with a tired grin, breaking up the sombre atmosphere.

Rebecca eyed her with feigned distaste. 'You didn't exactly give us a lot of time to change when you called,' she sniped. 'James can pick something up for me from the camping store.'

Sarah nodded and turned to her parents. 'We'll go past the fire station as well. If we can pick up a few good quality emergency radios, we can see who else is out there, and we should be able to keep in contact with each other if we need to separate. We'll keep it simple. We should be able to pack up and walk with it all, in case we have to abandon the cars.' Everyone nodded their assent. 'While we're at the shop, try to find some cars close by that can fit all of us and our supplies, and start packing three days' worth of water and food for each person. We'll come back here to install the radios, and plan how to get into the city. We'll have a better idea of what we're facing then too.'

It was growing dark by this time and, in the still oppressive heat, Sarah realised it could only be nervousness that caused a shiver to travel through her body, rattling its way through her bones. No one was very happy with her idea to take only James with her, even though she had argued that fewer people meant less chance of being seen, and greater odds of escape. Not to mention that they would need people to keep the house secure and prepare the cars for departure. In the end, Sarah hoisted Charlie out of Anica's arms and gave her to Rebecca, which worked to distract her a bit. She still appeared displeased at the idea of splitting the family up, regardless of how short a time it was for. James slid the gates open enough to allow them to slip through, closing them as Sarah unlocked her car, popping the boot open to move the largely unused bug-out bag to the front seat. The rest of the group crowded onto the narrow veranda, Rebecca clutching Charlie as though the child held the last vestige of her sanity in her tiny hands.

Sarah drove slowly down the street with her headlights off, relying on the remains of sunlight and the soft glow of the streetlights to guide her. As they turned left and crossed the railway tracks, the first visual evidence of the panicked public made itself known. In the middle of the intersection ahead, a large truck was turned onto its side and a line of empty cars filled the road behind it, beached on the nature strips where desperate drivers fought to pass. Sarah flicked the radio on, hoping for more information about what was going on.

'… have been receiving news from regional parts of Victoria that there seems to be a highly contagious virus causing people to behave in an erratic manner. These people seem to be driven to attack others violently and in most cases, fatally. The Prime Minister has released a statement to say that she has highly qualified people working on a solution.' There was a pause before the Prime Minister's voice came through the speakers, a soundbite from an address they had clearly missed. 'Australia's best and brightest at the CSIRO have been tasked with the momentous responsibility of ascertaining where this new threat has come from, and to make any and all efforts to restore peace to our country and our families.'

Sarah coasted to a stop, reaching a point in the road ahead that had been blocked off completely by a wall of traffic. She reversed and steered over to the side, aiming to move onto the opposite side of the road, but stopping when she saw that the blockage had extended there too, cutting them off completely.

The calm politician's voice was replaced with the first voice they had heard. 'People are advised to stay off the streets and lock their doors. The defence force has been mobilised in an attempt to contain the situation. More information will be sent to personal dev—'

James reached over and turned the radio off.

Sarah looked at him, annoyed. 'What w—?'

He slapped a hand over her mouth, his wide eyes glued on a spot beyond the windscreen. Sarah slowly turned her head in the same direction. A lone, silhouetted figure stood in the middle of the road, arms slightly outstretched to the side. It seemed to lean forward slightly as though straining to hear something in the distance.

'What do we do now?' James hissed. He still appeared to be frozen, unable to move.

Sarah looked around, anxiously grasping at ideas and discarding them just as quickly. Her mind flicked to the bag behind her seat, and the knife it held. She reached behind to pull it forward and pulled out the knife. She eyed the crowd in front of the car, voicing her thoughts softly.

'We don't know if it can see us, or how good its other senses are. There are enough cars between us and it, so we might be able to make it to the side of the road.'

James nodded and they reached simultaneously for their doors, which opened with a loud snick and the interior light flicked on. Their heads snapped to the front as though choreographed, and they fixated on the black figure in front of them, which now stared pointedly in their direction.

The figure let out a vicious snarl and hurled itself toward them. Sarah and James threw themselves out either side of the car, neither willing to be trapped in an unmoving coffin. Sarah stumbled and rolled under a removalists' truck that had stopped to the side of her, clutching the bag to her chest.

James found himself on the opposite sidewalk with no cover. Sarah watched in horror as the tall figure seemed to home in on him. James ran to the petrol station to his left and flung himself at the glass doors, hammering on them frantically without an answer.

Sarah crawled out of her position, breathing heavily. The pulse that hammered in her ears matched her brother's frenzied beating. She ran forward on silent feet, the small knife in her hand. As the approaching figure came to within a metre of her brother, she blindly reached out and snagged the handle of the windscreen squeegee beside her, swinging wildly. She hooked it around the greyish neck and hurled the creature backward toward the petrol pump, following it down to bury the blade in its ear. The thing kept moving, the knife too small to inflict the damage necessary to finish it off. She seized a petrol nozzle from the pump closest to her and jammed it into a milky eye, causing the creature to fall still.

Panting heavily Sarah turned away from the gruesome spectacle, staggering to the wall before throwing up. Distantly she heard James approach, but still flinched violently when he rested his hand on her back. He looked at the still figure and then at the squeegee that now lay discarded beside it.

'Were you planning on washing it to death?' His voice was strained with shock.

'Didn't you smell him? I'm sure he hasn't showered for a week,' she retorted weakly. They grinned wanly at each other, James walking over and prying the knife from its skull.

A low growling snapped their attention back to the present; James grasped her arm and pointed back at the street.

'There's more,' he hissed. The commotion had drawn the attention of what looked to be about fifteen creatures of various shapes and sizes. 'We need to find something better than a squeegee and that tiny knife for weapons.'

Sarah pointed to the far side of the street. 'There are factories over there; they should have something,' she suggested.

James shook his head and jerked his head directly across the road. 'The stock feed shop is closer and there's a spot in the fence you can get through,' he informed her, still eyeing the encroaching horde.

'How did you …' Sarah stopped, deciding not to pursue that thought. 'Actually, never mind. Let's go.'

They left the station, moving as quickly as they could in a crouch, throwing glances over their shoulders to check on the shambling group's progress. Fortunately the creatures seemed to remain focused on the station, the scene of the noise that had attracted them.

Sarah and James skirted the car and ducked under the truck that had hidden Sarah on her initial dash. She vaguely felt her arm catch on something sharp as they crawled under the truck. When they had made it to the other side, they could make out what appeared to be five of the creatures moving around the side of the car toward them.

'God, they look like they know where we are. How?' Sarah asked, feeling a cold chill up her spine as the dark shapes started to move away from the station, their attention now drawn to the truck where they hid.

'Could they be picking up our scent somehow?' James whispered, looking for a way to get to the fence behind them. 'Maybe their shitty sight means they have to rely on other senses to find food? It happens in humans, doesn't it?'

The creatures were rounding the end of the car now, forcing them to move. Sarah and James ran, hunched low, to the fence behind them. Sarah slowed to let her brother take the lead and followed him to a small gap in the fence. A quick pause for breath gave them a chance to look around the yard. There were a few sturdy looking cubby-houses in the front facing the road, presumably to hide the disassembled corpses of farmyard machinery and timber that took up the rest of the space.

Sarah turned to James, her mind still turning over the snatch of conversation from before. 'What could they be smelling? Sweat?'

'Possibly,' he mused. 'Or it could be that …' He gestured to her left arm where a gash had parted her skin, leaving a trail of black grease and blood that dripped down between her fingers.

Now the cut had been pointed out, she felt the pain running hot through her torn skin. She clasped a hand over the wound. It seemed to make sense—these things attacked human flesh. If the presence of blood in the water was enough to whip sharks into frenzy, the copper tang of blood might be enough to attract the attention of these new predators. She looked up at the growling figures that had made their way to the fence and had started to thread their fingers through the chain link mesh, reaching blindly toward their prey.

'Find a weapon and I'll go into the office. They may have a first-aid kit there,' she said, twisting herself off the ground and walking in the direction of the heavy wooden door to their right. James began to rummage through the pile of scrap metal in the yard as she started to haul the heavy door open. A scratching noise close to the floor inside made her pause.

'James,' she called softly. 'I might need you over here.'

He walked over, quickly grasping the situation when he heard the scratching. He raised the garden stake he had found above his head and nodded for Sarah to open the door. She pushed it open as quickly as gravity would allow, hearing a heavy thud as something fell to the floor behind the door. James swung down and pulled back as the yowl of a cat startled him. He laughed in relief as it darted out between them and they turned their attention back to the dark interior.

Sarah began to move inside, only to fall backward as a tall shadow detached itself from the wall and lurched toward her, arms out and grasping toward her eagerly. James jerked upwards, the bar that had fallen to rest beside his leg connecting with a heavy thwack to the skull of the not-so-dead man, sending him to the floor. The man laid still—no twitch, no last breath, just still. Sarah grimaced as she looked down at the creature; there was no way that thing hadn't been dead. The overall-clad man lay supine, a gaping hole where the smooth skin of his throat once was. She could see the stained bones of his vertebrae through the space, his eyes dry and milky-white fixed on the tin roof above them.

Sarah looked at her hands, surprised to see them tremble slightly. She clasped them together firmly to hide the shaking and moved silently to the desk, targeting the first aid box she could just make out, tucked away on the shelf. Washing her whole arm with the half empty bottle of Betadine, she pressed what little gauze there was onto the wound, cursing the lack of proper dressings in the cheap box. She wrapped a layer of gaffer tape around the gauze, hoping the extra padding would reduce any smell of the blood that might attract unwanted attention. Absently she slipped the tape into her backpack. A length of reinforcing bar, about a centimetre in diameter and 30 centimetres long, caught her attention, and she picked it up, swinging it to test its weight.

A triumphant yet muffled 'Thank you' drew her attention to James, who was standing in the corner holding aloft what looked like a pair of pliers.

'Wire cutters,' he said smugly, and moved toward the door, peering at the fence they had come through. The dead creatures were all still gathered there, but they had spread out enough that one or two had rounded the corner and were reaching along the next side the fence.

Knowing they had to leave before they were boxed in entirely, Sarah turned to James. 'Please tell me you have another way out.'

He waved the wire cutters in her face. 'I do now!' He skirted between the building and the junk piles, keeping inside the cover offered by the deep shadow. Sarah followed closely over the uneven ground. James huddled at the base of the last fence around the yard, cutting slowly so as not to make too much noise.

'Okay, quickly,' he said, pulling up a section of fence and moving it aside to let her go through. Then Sarah pulled the fence up on the other side so he could clamber after her into the next property.

The concreted area they found themselves in offered no hiding places. Keeping to the shadows again, they hugged the large building, holding their breath till they were at the gate on the far side. The gate was ajar and swung open easily on quiet hinges. Sarah whispered a prayer of thanks, and they stepped through. The road was separated from the commercial buildings by the wide grass strip that led onto the nature reserve at the end of the road, the length of which was drenched in shadows, the street lights having blown long ago.

The two crossed in silence, straining their ears for any movement or growling behind them. James slipped the wire cutters into his pocket and gripped his garden stake tightly as he walked quickly across the road and crouched low while he waited for Sarah to join him. Moving fast, they made their way down the road toward the narrow bridge that separated the grassy area from the protected wetland. Sarah paused at the mouth of the bridge, making a mental map of the area, trying to figure out the best route to take.

The road was a direct path to the fire station, but it was well lit, with multiple houses along the way. The wetland might have held fewer people, and it certainly provided some shadows to move through, but it was a longer way round, and who knew where those things were hiding?

Sarah nudged James's shoulder and started walking down the bridge toward the thick trees. The path guided them to where the trees thinned out and gave way to flat grass, bordered on one side by a high fence and sloping down to a moonlit lake on the other. The lack of cover sped their steps up a little as they rounded the fence and started up the grass slope leading to the road. They reached the top and Sarah saw the mistake in her choice immediately; to her right was a long driveway that led directly to the fast food strip along the freeway. The creatures that already crowded this path were numerous enough that the road beneath them was obscured. Most seemed to be swaying in place, rooted to the spot, although a few were walking aimlessly, following an unseen path in front of them. The closest zombie was about twenty metres away from them and, thankfully, facing in the other direction.

Keeping her eyes fixed on the massing horde, Sarah sidled to the left, anxious to leave the spotlight under which they had found themselves. At the end of the street, on the opposite side, stood the fire station, lit only by the bright lights of the self-serve car wash behind them. She moved down the street toward the solid walls of the car wash bays, snagging a finger in James's shirt and tugging to make sure he followed. Sarah threw herself down behind the first wall, James slumping beside her like a discarded rag. She peeked around the corner, trying to figure out a path across the street that would offer the most cover.

A slight scratching noise grated at her ears and she glanced around, looking for the source of the noise. The hulking shape of a four-wheel drive occupied one of the bays, with a small girl secured in a baby seat in the back. Her blonde pigtails were askew and she scratched mindlessly at the window, sightless eyes tracking random shadows. The front door of the four-wheel drive swung slightly in the hot breeze. James stared at the child in horror. Sarah had no doubt that in James's mind Charlie's face had superimposed itself over that of the slack-jawed toddler.

He stood abruptly and moved around the car. Sarah looked after him in shock. Surely he wasn't planning on releasing the child? A squelching thud shook her out of her confusion and she rushed to join her brother, clutching her iron bar like a security blanket. She found James standing over the body of a sallow skinned man in his mid-thirties, designer jeans in ruins, shirt ripped to expose a ragged hole in his abdomen, his head now split open with the force of James's swing. Sarah stepped over to him, draping an arm around his shoulder and turning him away.

'If anything happens … If I get bitten …'

Sarah understood what James left unsaid—the thought that this father could have attacked his daughter had made everything more harshly clear to him.

'Charlie has Bec,' she reassured him. 'And she has us. We won't let anything happen to them.' She left it there, unwilling to commit to a promise that might prove impossible to keep. Sarah could see James visibly pull himself together.

He glanced toward the looming car. 'What about her? I can't …' He stopped, unable to finish the thought.

'She's secure,' Sarah reassured him, walking over to shut the swinging door. 'She can't get out.'

James nodded, his posture straightening. The girl's eyes had fixated on him and she was growling softly.

Sarah's eyes narrowed in thought. 'Stay here a moment,' she muttered, and ducked below the car window, moving to the other side of the car. Once on the other side, she stood up quickly. The girl was still fixated on James. Sarah mouthed, 'Stay still' through the window. His face creased in confusion but he did as she requested. With the lack of movement, the girl lost interest, once again shifting her sightless eyes aimlessly about. Sarah waved a hand slowly in front of the glass. The girl's attention snapped to her and she lunged, stopped only by the seat belt that held her in place. Sarah took an involuntary step back and looked through the window to James. 'Now say something.'

'How about, what are you doing?' he asked softly. Again, the girl's head snapped around, her clawed hands scraping at the glass that separated them.

Sarah turned to check the road once more, hoping that the creatures were far enough away for her to test one more thing. She peeled back the tape on her arm and exposed a bloody corner of the gauze to the air. The girl spun around once more, chasing the scent of blood over the noise that had drawn her attention previously. Sarah wrapped her arm up again and ducked below the window, crouching as she moved behind the car to join James.

'Did you get what you needed?' he asked, frustrated at the waste of time.

'Yeah,' she hissed back, moving to the wall to check the road. 'I wanted to confirm what gets their attention. She was the safest way to do it.'

James frowned. 'It seemed a little uncouth. For the record,' he said, looking at the star-shaped bar in his hand, 'this is not a good weapon. My hands are already rubbed raw, and it's not easy to swing.'

'We'll find something better. They have to have something at the station.' Sarah gave him a fragile smile. Looking across at the fire station, she could see the garage doors directly in front of her, taking up twenty metres or so. The main entrance was glass, so it was easy to break into, but that would leave an open door for any zombies to enter once they were inside. There was a fence to the right side of the building with a small courtyard barely visible beyond. If they could get in there, there was a good chance they could open a window, and the fence should provide an adequate barrier. The milling zombies seemed to be drawn to movement, but if they couldn't see the movement, they couldn't track them, Sarah reasoned. She looked up and scowled at the fluorescent lights in the car wash that were drowning everything in a sea of white. The lights had to be turned off so they could cross the road, but if the lights went off suddenly, that might be enough to attract unwanted attention. She could see the main switch, secured behind a locked glass door in the second bay.

James crouched behind the wall beside her, wire cutters in hand, waiting for the go-ahead. A shattering of glass signalled the newly accessible control panel and he broke into a run for the fence just as the carwash was plunged into darkness. Whether it was as a result of the crash or the sudden darkness, a snarl went up among the zombies and Sarah could see the shadowy crowd starting to move in their direction. James fought shaking hands as he manoeuvred the wire cutters, opening up a passage through the fence. Sarah dived through the opened entrance and yanked the fence up enough to allow James to climb through. She let it fall closed behind him as the zombies began to fill the street between them and the carwash, some seemingly fixated on the change in light while others had apparently seen their movement and were now lined up along the fence, snarling and grasping at their prey.

James and Sarah scooted back into the narrow courtyard, out of the zombies' line of sight, breathing heavily as they pressed their backs against the wall to avoid looking at the horrific crowd. As they struggled to regain their breath, Sarah examined the windows that enclosed the courtyard. James had spotted a small door in the far end of the yard; he walked over to it and jiggled the handle, but it remained stubbornly secure. He slunk back to Sarah and flicked a hand, seemingly suggesting that she do something.

Sarah scowled at him. 'The onset of the zombie apocalypse does not mean I spontaneously gain the ability to pick locks,' she muttered through clenched teeth, turning her attention back to the windows. One seemed to have been left slightly ajar, not unusual given the December heat. She reached her hand in and pushed, sliding the window fully open. It was narrow, but still wide enough to offer access.

Neither of the two had been inside the fire station before and quickly found themselves disorientated in the darkness, stumbling around in the hallway hoping to happen across a door. A muted whoop brought Sarah's attention to the shadow that identified James's position at the end of the hall.

'They have a TV,' he whispered.

Sarah walked toward him, snapping the power switch on. The flickering light of the station-closed pattern lit up the room. A steady stream of elevator music grated on her nerves. She moved up beside James and pushed the volume button down till it was barely audible. She cycled through the other channels quickly, each end-of-transmission pattern further discouraging her. In desperation she flipped to Channel 31, hoping the public access channel might give her something to go on.

'... media blackout, the officials are trying to keep you in the dark ...' A mousy, slightly balding man in an ill-fitting suit sat close to the camera, filling the screen with his waxy, anxious face. His eyes jerked from side-to-side, as though looking for invisible hunters or predators lurking outside of the camera's scope. 'They say it's to prevent panic, but they don't want you to know what they did ... what they're still doing!' He desperately twisted his glasses in shaking fingers. 'There are bunkers! Tunnels all through the city! *They've* got themselves to safety, and have left you all at the mercy of those ravenous beasts!' The diminutive man stood up and started pacing, gesticulating wildly, at times leaving the screen entirely before rushing back to centre screen and lowering his voice to a grating rasp. 'Don't trust the military! They're protecting the people responsible for this mess, not you! No one's safe! The last I heard, Mildura has been hit bad and they've crossed state lines and are moving toward Wagga Wagga. Get out of the state if you can! The dingo fence is being reinforced. It's cutting the southeast away from the rest of Australia to contain the infection down here. Trust no one! There is …'

The ranting was cut off as James pulled the plug, sending the room into darkness once more.

'Conspiracy nut?' James asked.

Sarah looked as though she were about to agree, then stopped. 'Last week zombies were a conspiracy,' she mused.

James looked at her doubtfully. 'Are you saying sweat-pit McGee might not be talking crazy?'

'Not at all—the man's nuts.' She smiled. 'Just saying, we really don't know what's right anymore. We have to be careful who we trust. The government may very well be "mobilising forces to contain this infection".' She crooked her fingers to signal the quote. 'But we don't know how far it's spread, or even if there is a government to send them out anymore. We haven't heard anything really. Although …' she mused. 'The dingo fence does cut the south off. If they have started reinforcing it, maybe we just have to get that far?'

She shook her head to focus, pushing the thought to the side. They moved together back into the corridor, quickly locating the main floor. Faint moonlight spilled in through the high windows and provided a vague sense of shadows in the large six-truck wide area. The first thing Sarah noted was the absence of all but one truck, most likely due to the number of 000 calls that had flooded the emergency services. The reason that the lone truck had been left behind became apparent as she rounded its tail. The bulky pants of a firefighter's uniform were visible, lying out past the far end. She peeked around the corner briefly, whipping her head back as she assimilated what she had seen. A fully equipped firefighter had his head bent low over his fallen comrade. It looked as though he were checking on his wellbeing, if not for the half-chewed arm he had raised to bloodied lips, yellowing teeth worrying at the splintered bone.

Sarah peeked back around the side of the truck to where James knelt, peering under the chassis at the stained uniforms. She crooked a finger to call him over and pointed at the metal bar in his hand, at the rebar she held in her other hand, and then toward the corner of the truck. James nodded and they moved in tandem around the side of the truck. The creature snapped his head up, the muffled sound of footsteps enough to alert it to new company. Sarah whipped her rebar forward, snapping the zombie's head backward, allowing for James to stab his bar sharply forward, penetrating the soft skin beneath the jaw and through the soft palette of the sinus cavity, embedding it deep in the brain and stilling the creature permanently.

'Let's have a proper look around,' she muttered, not wanting to be surprised by more lurking zombies. James softly walked to the offices lining the back wall. Sarah looked at the top of the truck and hurled herself up the ladder to get a better vantage point.

Turning in a full circle, she took in the evidently rapid evacuation of the station. Cupboard doors hung open, the door to the office slightly ajar. She watched carefully as James pushed it open. He paused, looking beyond the door into the room before walking in. She started to climb down the ladder, pausing halfway as her eye caught the unusual shape of what appeared to be a pry bar tucked under the ladder. She reached through, barely able to touch the bar, snagging her nail on a small part that jutted out to the side and pulling slowly, so as not to let go of it. As she pulled it close enough to grasp, she yanked it backward violently, nearly pinwheeling to the floor below, catching the rungs just in time.

'James,' she called out softly.

He poked his head back through the door and she held up the new tool.

'Keep an eye out for more of these, they might come in handy.'

James nodded to signify that he had heard and disappeared again into the office.

Turning her attention to the open cupboards, she flipped them open one by one. They seemed to have been cleared out for the most part. Sarah returned to the truck and walked to the driver's side door, opening it to look for the onboard radio. Her hopes sank as she realised that the radio was secured in the solid panel in front of her, locked amongst the myriad cables, knobs and buttons. She had no idea where the radio was or how to get to it if she could isolate it.

James came out of the office, a green box cradled in his arms. There were several dials on the front with a handheld mouthpiece secured to the side, and small black panels that looked out of place secured to the top.

'I found something,' he said, not looking up from the green box. 'I don't think its official equipment, but it looks like a short-wave. Did you have any luck in the truck?'

Sarah shook her head. 'No, that's all we have.' She indicated the box, taking in his subdued appearance. 'Are you okay?'

He looked up at her, his eyes distant. 'I tried to call Rebecca,' he mumbled. 'It looks like the phone companies have caught up with the drama. I can't get through, not to her, not to Mum and Dad.' He looked back to the radio.

Sarah pulled out her phone, needing to confirm what James had said for her anxious mind. The signal bars were still there, mocking her with their full coverage. She called her Mum's house.

A tinny voice apologised for being unable to connect her call at this time. She frowned, calling her Mum's mobile, then her Dad's, receiving the same message each time.

'It might just be that the servers are busy. There would be thousands of people trying to call,' she reminded James morosely, slipping the phone back into her pocket and turning to the radio, still cradled in James's arms. She rested her hand on the plastic cover. 'This was a good find.' She knew the words were empty, but said them anyway. 'It means we can still communicate.'

'Not without another one,' he reminded her. 'There's only one here.'

'We're still heading to the camping store. They should have one there. Plus,' she added as an afterthought, 'other people using these might have information about what's out there.'

James seemed to brighten up a little. 'So, let's figure out how to get there,' he pressed, eager to move on.

# Chapter Four

Not long after James had left with Sarah, Charlie began to fuss in Rebecca's arms, seeming to instinctively recognise that part of her family was missing. Rebecca paced from the living room to the kitchen, crossing the short span so many times that she knew Anica had started checking surreptitiously for a trough in the timber floor. The feelings of helplessness and anxiety clashed viciously, creating an internal maelstrom that refused to allow any offers of comfort. With her parents stuck in the middle of a hostile city, and the realisation that she was unable to do anything to physically assist her husband or her sister, Rebecca was left with a hopelessness that threatened to smother her.

A car alarm sounded in the adjacent street and she jumped violently, startling a surprised cry out of her daughter. Alex walked to the front window, peering through the twilight beyond the glass. The street stared back with eerie stillness. A second alarm sounded, this time closer, the clashing lights visible through the thick trees that covered the vacant ground across the road from the house. Alex moved away from the window and quickly pulled the blinds shut.

'Turn the lights off!' Everyone stared at him, stunned into immobility. 'Now!' he insisted, and everyone scurried to hit the switches, plunging the room into darkness. Alex's fingers parted the blinds enough for him to peer through them. He spoke softly to the room behind him. 'There's something out there.'

Rebecca and Anica parted the fabric slightly at the side of the window, eager to see what had riled up the usually placid man.

A shadow lurched forward on unsteady feet, stumbling forward into a pool of light, allowing the onlookers their first glimpse of the new horror that haunted their lives. The creature was dressed in a Safeway uniform, her once blonde hair now a matted red, and her arms were held slightly away from her body as though she would lose her balance at the slightest provocation. The most predominant feature on her, however, was the gaping hole where her jaw had once been. The mandible appeared to have been torn off, leaving her with a ghastly appearance.

Rebecca gasped, feeling the blood drain from her face. She wavered slightly on her feet and clutched Charlie to her tightly, burying the child's uncomprehending eyes into her soft shirt, trying to shelter her from the horror outside. Nell squeaked from the lower corner of the window, where she had jostled her way through to see what everyone was fixated on. Both of her hands flew up to cover her mouth as she scurried back from the window. Alex and Anica moved closer to each other, his arm coming up to rest across her shoulders in a protective gesture. Three sets of eyes tracked the path of the figure as it moved beyond their line of sight to where it was blocked by the tall fence separating them from their neighbours.

The shrill ring of a mobile shattered the stillness in the room and Rebecca thrust Charlie into Anica's arms, racing to her bag to shut the sound off. She glanced up toward the window with a terror-filled expression etched on her face. A quick glance at her phone as she turned it to silent revealed her mother's name. She moved to the bathroom in the back of the house and called the number back quickly. Holding the phone in shaky fingers, she whispered, 'Mum? Are you okay? Where's Ben? Where are you?' The strong voice of Rebecca's mother Cass seemed to soothe some of her anxiety.

'We're fine for now,' Cass said softly, her voice echoing slightly. 'We're currently in an old tunnel under the hospital. The nurses evacuated as many as they could down here. It's huge, but crowded at the moment ...' she trailed off before murmuring softly, 'There were so many left behind though.'

Rebecca ached for her mother, unable to do anything more than offer platitudes over the phone. 'Have you heard from Dad or Laura?' she asked, desperate for reassurance.

'We called them just before we called you—they made it to the fort. Apparently there were military trucks combing the street and they managed to get on one of those. There's a temporary refugee camp being set up there.'

Rebecca sighed, relief evident in her voice.

'There was talk of a safe house being set up in the Geelong jail, as well as a few other places through the city,' Cass continued. 'This tunnel connects with the hospital across the road, so the professionals are still trying to work out how to get us up there safely. I'm sure they'll figure something out.'

Rebecca could hear the note of doubt in her mother's words, even as she reassured her, and her gut twisted. She frowned as she noticed Anica gesturing to her and looked up. Her mother-in-law's face was drawn and white, her attention flicking between Rebecca and the living room window.

'I have to go, Mum,' she said quietly. 'Stay safe ... I'll talk to you later,' adding the words 'I hope' in her head. She hung up and slowly joined the small group in the living room.

All eyes were locked on the window and Rebecca drew the curtain back just enough to see out, before she dropped it back into place. The creature they had been watching now stood at the solid gates of the house, a low wet growl bubbling out of its throat.

'It followed the noise,' Anica whispered, her eyes fixed on the hands grasping at the gate. Her voice was absent of accusation but this didn't stop the feeling of guilt that niggled at the back of Rebecca's mind. The clawed hands seemed to trace the lines of the gate as though looking for a way in.

'What do we do?' Nell's trembling voice peeped, looking to Alex for direction.

'I can't really claim any experience in this field,' he retorted dryly, one eyebrow raised.

'We kill it. Quietly. James has made me sit through enough of those bloody movies to know that we can't leave it outside,' Rebecca stated with a decisiveness that she knew she didn't feel.

Alex stood and moved to the kitchen, looking through the draws and picking up knives. 'If this *is* like all those ridiculous movies,' he grimaced, as though struggling to admit it, 'we have to destroy the brain. That's usually what they say keeps it active, right? No way of knowing which part of the brain though. What if it's the wrong part and it acts like a lobotomy? Lobotomy patients don't die; some have normal lives. It might have no effect on the zombies.' His disconnected thoughts pulled his mind in different directions. He walked back to the living room to the hanging tools by the fireplace. He hefted the poker in his hand, feeling the weight and the swing and nodded. 'Okay, so we'll destroy the whole brain, just to be sure.' Poker in hand, he moved to the back door, deciding not to announce his presence too early and surrender the element of surprise. He walked down the narrow path along the side of the house, heading steadily for the front yard. He reached for the low gate with an outstretched hand and, breathing a quick prayer, pushed it open on silent hinges.

The garden bed he walked out onto was slightly raised, sitting about seventy centimetres above the driveway. The line of bushes that provided privacy from passersby was thick enough to offer cover, as he ducked into a crouch and moved closer to the fence. As he craned his neck to peer through the leaves, he could make out the creature's head, barely an arm's length away from him, but too low for him to be able to do anything from this angle. At this distance, he could make out the yellowish grey tinge to her skin and a foul smell choking the air around her. Gagging slightly on a necessary breath, he stepped off the garden wall into direct sight of the unwholesome creature. He raised his arm and swung but misjudged his aim and hit the iron bars, the deafening clang reverberating up his arms and shattering the surrounding stillness. The zombie's milky eyes were now locked on his movements and a dirty, questing arm reached for him insistently. He grabbed the offered arm and yanked, slamming her head into the hard bars. She snarled, not affected by the impact. He repeated the action, again pulling the yielding flesh to meet the unyielding bars. This time he held tight, keeping her pressed against the gate, her torn, bloodied face pushed hard into the gap. Alex thrust the poker hard, tearing through the soft tissue at the back of her throat and pushing through the unprotected brain, penetrating the top of her skull.

Panting heavily, Alex threw the corpse away from him, the poker still lodged in place by the shattered bone. She landed heavily, one arm flung onto the road behind her, and Alex turned away, not wishing to look at the mess. He looked down at his hands, now sticky and red, walking into the house and silently making his way to the bathroom. Turning the taps on, he slumped in the steaming shower and let the tears flow.

The living room was silent. Even Charlie seemed to feel the gravity of the situation and was snuggled quietly in her mother's arms.

Rebecca pulled her phone out, shooting off a text to James and staring at the screen uncomprehendingly when it reported it was unable to send the message. She tried to dial his number, hoping it was just a glitch, but was turned away by a voice informing her that she was unable to make calls at this time. A quick check of the other phones in the house revealed the same outcome. Even the landline seemed to mock her attempts and she threw the phone to the timber floor, watching the battery escape its plastic shell and skitter beneath the table. She glared at the traitorous mobile phone that had been working fine not even an hour before. Rebecca threw a soft blanket on the floor, bordering it with pillows before placing Charlie down and standing back to look at the small group.

'We know the house is fairly safe, but if we can't be out there helping, let's be in here making sure the place is secure. Nothing too big or noisy, just make sure there isn't any easy access into the house.' Her voice had got its strength back and she was proud of the way it refused to tremble. 'Mum, can you make sure the side gate is completely secured and just check that there's no easy way to climb over from the side or the front?' She turned to a white-faced Nell. 'Dad should be out soon but let him take his time. For now, I need you to watch Charlie for me while we're outside. Can you do that?' Nell nodded, cowed by the protective mother.

Anica had already started toward the door and, with everyone distracted, Rebecca grabbed a notebook from the desk by the window. She scribbled a quick note, swapped her skirt for pants and high heels for a pair of runners out of Anica's cupboard, and followed her out. Anica had moved along the side fence toward the front before Rebecca pulled herself onto the roof of the shed via a stunted fruit tree.

She jumped over the back fence that separated their house from the neighbours. No lights were on in the house and the only dogs she heard belonged to the next house down, so in silence she walked the length of the fence, checking for weak spots. The shed behind Anica's house had long ago been converted to a separate house, giving a solid secondary wall as added security. With this in mind, she had chosen to check that fence first, knowing it would take the least time to complete, and giving her a chance to implement her hastily made plan without having to waste time explaining it to the group. The scribbled note she had left prominently on the kitchen bench would tell them what she was doing and why, bypassing the inevitable argument that would have followed. This way she could be assured of her daughter's continued safety while she pursued the safety of the rest of her family, who huddled amongst strangers who held no loyalty to them.

Rebecca crept around the side of the house, grabbing a small axe from the lean-to shed beside it. The usually innocuous street was dark and suddenly intimidating. She paused at the low brick fence that bordered the yard. The abandoned streets seemed foreign. From what she could see, no cars were piled up on the back roads and walking to the city would take hours. She moved beside the only car she could see in the street and tested the door, not surprised to find it locked. She leant against the car and swung the heavy head of the axe against the rear window. The sound of shattering glass was amplified in the still night. Rebecca froze, ears straining for any indication that she had been heard.

As her heart rate began to slow once more and the tension seemed to bleed from her shoulders, she heard a slight shuffle from a garden across the street. Quickly, Rebecca hurtled over the wall behind her and shuffled backward into the short bushes that sprawled along the fence. She stopped moving, hearing a growl roll through the air around her. Her eyes flicked up, just in time to see two figures lurch on unsteady feet toward the car, their ghastly faces pale and hollow in the milky moonlight. The bush around her seemed to shift and she strangled the scream that leapt to her throat as a large hand clamped itself over her mouth. Rebecca swung her elbow sharply backward, hearing the huff of air behind her as she connected with a solid mass before a low rumble whispered in her ear.

'I'm not going to do anything, but keep moving around like a bloody rabbit and they will.'

Rebecca froze and turned her head slightly, unable to get a clear view of the man behind her. From his shadowed form, he was a little taller than her, but his features remained obscured by the shadows.

'Is this your house?' she whispered, and then looked back at the car in horror. 'Did I just try to steal your car?'

'It's my sister's house, and she won't be needing the car anymore. Do you even know how to hot—' He broke off suddenly as the nearest zombie raised his head and started to turn in their direction. Its gaping mouth was open, showing discoloured teeth. A second zombie reached the far side of the car and began to run his hand over its side, leaving a trail of blood on the white paint. His other arm had been reduced to a bloodied stump that ended just below the shoulder; the frayed remnants of a blue shirt and ragged clumps of flesh spoke of forceful removal, though the pain no longer seemed to register.

Rebecca looked on in shock as the first zombie spun fully toward her with unseeing eyes, somehow accurately picking their location. He released a guttural snarl that shook Rebecca's spine. The man behind her rose gracefully to his feet, snapping out a metal police baton in one smooth motion. Both zombies stepped forward eagerly, three hands grabbing at the air between them.

'Time to put that axe to use,' said the man, his eyes not leaving the creatures before him. He jumped over the low wall, darting to the side as the first zombie lunged at him, arms outstretched, spit coating the skin around his gaping mouth. The baton whipped out forcefully, making a satisfying *thunk* on contact with its skull and changing its trajectory, sending the creature sprawling to the ground. As Rebecca stepped into the street, he moved on to the next threat, sweeping its legs from beneath it in a fluid motion that spoke of years of training, and drove the heel of his boot through the bridge of its nose, shattering the cartilage and destroying the tissue and brain matter behind it.

Rebecca had swung her axe down, parting the skull of the first felled zombie with the sharp edge of the axe and now struggled not to throw up as she tried to pull the wedge from where it had stuck fast in the bone. The ruined head jerked up toward her with every yank. Her companion walked over and rested his boot on the neck, pulling the axe free with a wet crack and handing it back to her.

'Quickly, in the car,' he ordered. 'There's bound to be more responding to the noise any minute.' He pulled a set of keys from his pocket and unlocked the door. Rebecca fell into the passenger seat and closed her eyes as the stranger sat behind the wheel and turned the engine over, pulling quickly away from the curb.

'I'm Seth,' he said, glancing over at Rebecca.

'Rebecca,' she responded, gulping at the air that streamed into the car through the broken window. 'Sorry about the car,' she winced, looking at the shattered back window behind him.

'Meh.' He shook off the apology. 'Air conditioning was sorely needed in this heap.'

Rebecca fought back her nausea and looked over at him, able to make out his features for the first time. Thick black hair fell carelessly over light grey eyes; his strong nose and jaw gave his profile a trustworthy, commanding air. He looked to be a born leader and, with his obvious skill and training, she would be surprised if it wasn't the case.

'Where are you headed?' she asked.

'Back to base. I'm visiting from Simpson Barracks. The plan is to make it back there and report for duty.'

'Air force?' she asked. 'My sister-in-law is on the Adelaide base.'

'Army,' he enunciated clearly. 'No satin sheets here.' He grinned across at her.

'Sorry,' she laughed back. 'No offence meant.'

'Just don't forget it!' His playfulness contrasted sharply with the scene they had just left. 'Where are you headed?' he asked, and Rebecca sobered up slightly.

'My parents are trapped in the hospital. Apparently there are tunnels below that they managed to get to. It sounded crowded when I finally got hold of them.' She looked out the window at the dark streets. 'Do you have any idea what's going on?' she asked tentatively.

Seth was pensive. 'Not really. It was all very hush-hush you know? Regular need-to-know bullshit and all that.' He paused, either gathering his thoughts or debating the pros and cons of too much information being in civilian hands. 'About a month ago, a group of our scientists were requested to move up here to Geelong—something about a new experimental vaccine that went wrong. Our specialists were sent in to work with the team here, see what went wrong, what they could salvage, and what they would have to do to correct it.' He scoffed slightly. 'I was already approved for leave, and left soon after that. Next thing I hear, I'm getting a call ordering me back to base. That was early this morning. I never got the chance to leave the city but I'll give it my best shot.' He shrugged and trailed off, pulling over to the side of the road, a dubious look on his face as he glanced down at the normally busy road below.

A quick look outside told Rebecca they had parked on the bridge that passed over the freeway leading to the waterfront and curled back to lead people into the heavy traffic of the Princes Highway. Rebecca looked at the sea of traffic that blocked the Melbourne bound lanes completely and back at Seth.

'There's a reserves base in Geelong. Do you have to go all the way back?' A small part of her brain berated her for showing this weakness to a stranger.

'Reserves is hardly the same thing.'

'Some of my friends are in the reserves here,' she said defensively.

Seth held his hands up. 'Not poking fun, just pointing out that there is a difference between regular and reserves. We have more training and better toys for instance.' He smirked and she poked him hard, making him jump in surprise. 'Ahh, just joking.'

Rebecca rolled her eyes and hesitantly opened the door. Seth raised his hand as though to stop her but pulled it back wordlessly.

'Good luck,' he said, throwing her a salute and driving on to the freeway.

She watched as his taillights sped down the wrong side of the road, taking advantage of the empty inbound lanes as he drove toward Melbourne. Rebecca turned and walked over the rest of the bridge, making her way toward the roundabout that looked down onto the deceptively serene waters of Corio Bay.

The moon had reached its peak and was providing a gentle light as she walked the quiet path above the water. She could see the outline of the city where it sat nestled against the curve of the bay against the night sky. A steady drone seemed to ooze from between the distant buildings and settle like a dense fog in her ears. The axe hung heavy in her hand and she thought back to the zombies at the car. Seth had needed to yank it free for her. If she was to be caught in a real fight on her own, it could mean her death. She needed to find a proper weapon. Her mind conjured up an image of Seth's baton, blunt and deadly. That's what she needed to look for. She pulled up a rough mental map, struggling to recall the shops that littered the area around her. There was only a hotel along the waterfront and, while it might have something to offer in the way of weapons, it also held the potential of tourist zombies spilling out at her. The thought turned the idea sour. She could vaguely remember Sarah talking about a tyre shop off Mercer Street, which ran parallel to where she stood.

That would probably have more to offer in the way of tools that could be adapted to something she could use.

Leaving the bay behind, she moved silently down the road as she made her way deeper into the summer night. The green concrete building crept into view around the corner, marking the end of the residential buildings on the small street. The lack of movement so far had her nerves strung tight, expecting to be beset at every shadow she passed. Even for the early hour the streets were unnaturally silent. Choosing not to question her good fortune, Rebecca approached the garage quietly. The front of the shop was a wall of glass with racks of tyres concealing the room behind it. To the right of this, two garage doors marked the mechanics' domain. Rebecca walked the length of the shopfront, looking for a way in. She wouldn't be able to secure the windows again afterwards, and the falling wall of tyres would undoubtedly draw attention to her location. She shuddered, not wanting to think about the number of zombies that would be crowding the city at the end of the street.

Following the driveway skirting the shop, she found herself in a cramped courtyard framed with four brick walls, one of which barely managed to peep over the top of a dam of discarded tyres, which filled the yard and butted up to the rear wall of the tyre shop. Narrow windows were set into the wall starting a metre from the ground. Rebecca pulled one of the larger tyres across to the wall under a high window and stepped up, peering through the dust-coated window into the room beyond. The black objects scattered through the room identified it as an office. It looked to be empty of people, but even with the axe in hand she hesitated. If there were something in there, a smashed window would be sure to bring them to investigate. She looked up at the roof. It offered a flat space that should be secure enough to rest on. Piling a couple more tyres onto her initial platform and tucking the axe handle into the waistband of her borrowed pants, she held tightly to the narrow gutter that clung to the wall, and hoisted herself onto the tin roof, wincing at the metallic groan. Pulling the axe out of her pants, she leant over the edge and swung down, letting gravity pull the iron sharply down against the thin glass, shattering it.

A scrabbling noise from within the dark room was the first indication that she had company. A low groan assaulted her ears and she scrambled backward on the roof, taking her out of the line of sight. A loud crash inside caused her to jump. The creaky roof protested her sudden movement and she scooted forward, just to the point where she was able to see the lower edge of the window and part of a desk that sat in front. The desk was partially covered by what looked to be a blue scrap of material. It moved as she watched, reaching out to grab at the window frame, the remnants of glass cutting deep into unfeeling skin. The creature laboriously fell over the bottom frame of the low window and spilled itself onto the scattered tyres that covered the ground below. She watched as it stumbled across the uneven courtyard, waiting to hear if there were any more zombies inside.

Finally deciding that the creature had been alone inside the building, Rebecca let her breath out slowly. Drawing on years of pre-motherhood gym training, she spread her arms along the length of the roof and leant forward. Watching the creature stumble further into the courtyard, she let the distance increase before leaning forward and, like the axe before her, let gravity carry her over the side of the roof and into the glassless window below her. She let go as her knees hooked the frame, holding a whimper in as the remaining glass shards carved shallow fissures into her skin as she fell onto the desk below. A roar from outside alerted her to the fact that her acrobatic prowess had not gone unnoticed by the creature outside and she scrambled backward off the desk as it tripped toward her. She tipped the desk up onto its narrow edge, turning the solid side to the open window and shoving it firmly against the empty frame. She turned to the room behind her, eager to put more than an unsteady desk between her and the desperate predator. The walls to either side were covered by shelves and filing cabinets filled with car manuals and folders, offering no assistance in the way of defence; the door to the room was in the centre of the opposite wall, with a narrow bay of old fashioned, wind-out windows filling the space between the top of the door and the roof.

A quick test of the handle informed her that it was locked and the deadbolt secured, presumably by the overall-clad owner that now pawed at the blocked window behind her. A relocated filing cabinet allowed Rebecca to reach the window comfortably and she wound it open. The window angled out into the corridor, just wide enough for her to slip through. She carefully climbed on top of the metal case, holding the window to remain steady. She hoisted herself up to sit backward on the window ledge, feet still hanging into the office, and swung her legs awkwardly over the chain that held the window ajar. Sucking in sharply she slithered through the narrow gap and into the hallway beyond.

Rebecca rocked back to lean against the door, taking advantage of the short respite. The hallway she found herself in housed three doors that she could see, aside from the door she leant against; two of which were across from her, and one directly to her right at the far end of the hallway. The first door opened with a slight protest under her hand, the whine of the hinge causing Rebecca to wince. Unable to hear any movement from behind the door, she pushed it open and walked into what appeared to be a garage, the two large roller doors she had seen from outside providing a grimy wall at the far end. Benches and toolboxes lined the room around the two car lifts in the centre of the floor. She pawed through each of them, looking for an appropriate weapon that she could realistically use. Finally she settled on a long bar with a socket wrench on one end and a bevelled point on the other.

A heavy *thunk* and squelch from the hallway jerked her attention to the door behind her. Was there another person here she hadn't seen? Another zombie? The jangle of keys rattled through the walls. Perhaps there was another employee who had locked himself behind the door she hadn't yet checked? She clenched her newly appropriated bar tightly and stepped toward the door, raising the bar to shoulder height, ready to strike. The door opened slowly and she brought the bar down firmly across her body only to have it caught and yanked from her grasp. Her damp hands betrayed her in favour of the unidentified person as it was ripped from her grasp.

'Are you going to attack me every time we meet?' Seth's strong voice reverberated through the tense air.

'Seth?' Rebecca looked at him, shock smeared across her face. 'I could have killed you!'

Seth looked pointedly at the bar in his possession and Rebecca flushed, shooting him a glare that must have lacked conviction if his smirk was any indication.

Rebecca changed the subject brusquely. 'Aren't you supposed to be halfway to Watsonia by now?'

'I got as far as Little River. Apparently the idea to use the other side of the road was not a unique one. Both sides of the road are completely impassable.'

Seth used the ensuing silence to look closer at the woman in front of him. Rebecca looked haggard, her hands shaking at her sides. Blood oozed from the gashes in her legs and he guided her to a stool against the wall, pushing her gently to get her to sit down.

'How did you find me?' she asked. Seth had located the first-aid kit and was kneeling on the floor with her leg propped on his knee as he prodded delicately at the skin, looking for any glass that may have been left behind. He wiped the cuts down with the antiseptic swab he'd pulled from the kit, and wound a soft bandage around the torn skin.

'I followed the main road and happened to be passing the tyre shop when you broke the glass.' Her legs were now swathed in the clean white material, the skin of her calves having been torn up on both legs. 'I assume you still intend to find your family?' he asked rhetorically, a soft, resigned sigh escaping him.

Rebecca glared, daring him to find fault with familial loyalty, but he just nodded silently.

'First, you need to sleep.' He cut off the protest he could see forming on her lips. 'For the moment, your family is safe, while you are exhausted and injured.' His eyes drifted to her torn and bloody pant legs. 'You saw that thing out the back, how it responded to the scent of your blood. You can't expect to fight them off while you're trying to keep yourself upright.'

As though awaiting verbal permission, the weight of exhaustion that she had been keeping at bay crashed over her. She looked around, hoping to at least land on a flat surface as she fell.

Seth chuckled and placed a supporting hand below her elbow, guiding her to the door. 'There are couches in the next room; they'll be softer than the concrete floor.'

Robbed of her ability to form a coherent argument, she allowed him to lead her forward. A sharp metallic jangle assaulted her senses as he pulled out a ring of keys from his pocket and unlocked the next door.

Seth smiled. 'I figured our friend in the courtyard wouldn't be needing them any longer.' Rebecca dragged tired eyes up to lock his with a flat stare. Seth swung the door open, bowing her through flippantly.

They slumped through into a room bordered with stacked tyres. 'The showroom,' her fatigued brain surmised. Two small couches and a tyre-shaped beanbag sat in the middle of the room, just past a chest-high counter littered with papers, calendars and novelty maps. Seth whipped the cushions off the couches and threw them behind the counter. Rebecca blinked in confusion.

'How is a bare couch more comfortable than a concrete floor?' she asked, staring at the exposed straps in the couch seat.

Seth patted the top of the desk. 'It's no concrete bunker, but this will at least offer better protection than the glass walls.'

Lacking the strength to do anything but agree, Rebecca threw her weary body onto the scattered cushions and directly fell asleep.

Seth stared down at the softly snoring figure. 'So, I'll take first watch then?' he asked the senseless girl. Walking back to the door beside the locked office, he fixed a strong coffee and took it back to the front room, seating himself in the beanbag to settle in for his watch, his baton resting against his knees. A glance to the clock behind him mocked his tired eyes, its black hands indicating 0230.

# Chapter Five

Sarah and James made tediously slow progress as they worked their way toward the yellow building in front of them. The camping store they had highlighted on the map was within sight, down the highway toward Geelong's CBD. An unknown number of the infected creatures milled through the streets in between. Scattered cars were dotted through the car park in which they had found themselves. James had been eager to continue the journey on four wheels and had started to move toward the nearest car. Sarah pulled him back quickly, reminding him that the zombies seemed to be drawn toward noises and, no matter how safe they may be inside the car, there was no guarantee they would be able to make it out again. And this was assuming they would even be able to get the car started with their limited car-jacking skills, gained from snatches of movies and television shows.

A pointed finger pulled Sarah's attention toward the next building in their block. Propped against a bike rack along the side of the building were three bikes, two of them full-sized and a child-sized one with a floral basket secured to the handlebars. Not allowing her mind to dwell on the fate of the previous owners, she gestured for James to stay behind her. Sarah moved across the open car park in a hunched crouch, eyes skittering in every direction, watching for movement around her as she crossed the empty car park. Aside from a threatening cat, she made it to the bikes quickly. She spun around to flash a grin at James, who made an impatient 'hurry up' gesture, as he followed her across to the bike rack. Sarah gingerly lifted the smaller bike from where it rested on the others. A large clattering had her hair standing on end again. The two smaller bikes had balanced precariously on their kick-stands and, once the one thing holding them upright had been taken away, gravity had taken hold and dropped them to the concrete, taking their hope of a quiet, uneventful escape with them.

Sarah stood up quickly and grabbed the nearest bike. She pulled it upright and James snatched up the second bike. He opened her backpack, shoving in the rebar, wire cutters and fireman's tool, not bothering to zip it closed completely, and jumped onto the last bike, holding the radio tight in his hand. They took off, frantically peddling toward the freeway. As their front tyres hit the road, the dull, droning moan pushed its way into their ears once more. In the service station ahead and to the right, Sarah could see the silhouette of a solitary stumbling figure moving slowly toward them.

'I hate that sound!' James panted. 'How does a dead person even make that noise? Their lungs are useless!'

Sarah's years of ignoring bikeriding in favour of walking were catching up quickly as she struggled to catch her breath to answer him, eyes stuck on the shambling creature.

'They keep—*huh*—sniffing. The air that gets—*pffhuh*—sucked in has to come out somehow—*godhelpme*—' Sarah reasoned before falling silent again, her concentration torn between keeping the unfamiliar bike steady and moving, and the figure that drew steadily closer as they rode. There was a dip in the road coming up that would give them a slight push to increase the distance between them. Sarah sped up a little in eagerness and let the bike coast downhill with a small, relieved smile. The zombie was now fifty metres behind them, the distance increasing with every second. As they flew over the hill, Sarah's smile dissolved.

The downward slope was fine and clear, but on the other side of the dip, the road went uphill before veering sharply to the left, the hillside strewn with the horrific remains of fleeing residents.

Sarah looked down on the carnage before her. She could see what must have been at least two cars that had taken the corner at a speed too great for the curve, causing an accident that involved about five cars if the debris was anything to go by. The tight bank of cars behind the pile-up had effectively sealed off this exit out of the city, potentially more depending on how far back the pile-up stretched. What had sent Sarah's heart to her feet, however, were the hundreds of figures she could see milling about the cars, the low, steady hum of the collective moans setting her teeth on edge.

Sarah and James veered in unison toward the side of the road. The thick bushes that grew there would hopefully give them some semblance of cover to collect their thoughts. Sarah threw her bike down beside an already prone James. He turned so he could open the pack and get the weapons out. He handed her the fireman's tool.

'The rebar must have fallen out,' he winced apologetically.

Sarah waved it off, grasping the tool and shifting forward so she could see the road through the thick foliage that hid them. The store was three kilometres further down the road and in plain view, but the sea of moaning, shambling creatures made the distance seem so much greater. Sarah closed her eyes, trying to draw up her memory of the area. She had driven this road for years, but in the early morning, with this new threat spreading death over the city, the road and its surroundings seemed to morph into something alien and menacing. For the most part, the road was skirted by the scrub they were hiding in, with a small storm water drain running under the road about a kilometre away. Their cover unfortunately didn't reach the camping store, as the commercial area started a block before it after a service road. But if they could reach the road they would be that much closer to their goal.

They made their way cautiously through the bushes until they reached the dry ditch that funnelled under the wide road and started to climb up the other side. A scrabbling noise brought them up short and they frantically looked around, trying to find the source of the noise. At the end of the drain on the other side of the road they could make out the small shape of a figure pulling himself down the side of the gully, head first. The cause of its awkward posture became apparent as it reached the ground and Sarah was able to see that the figure ended abruptly below the waist.

She poked James to prompt him to move and they pulled themselves up the incline as an echoing growl barrelled through the concrete tube, the amplified sound spilling out both ends of the concrete pipe. As though a dinner bell had rung, every zombie, walking, crawling and slithering, had turned and started moving toward the sound, splitting off from the group to answer both sides of the echo.

'Run!' James hissed. They took off for the fence line, keeping in a low crouch to stay as close to the line of bushes as they could. They sprinted toward the buildings at the end of the fence. So far, the creatures seemed to remain focused on the tunnel where the echoed moan had come from. Sarah hoped that the sound would be enough to distract them from the shadowy figures running down the exposed side of the fence.

She reached the fence line first, breathing heavily, cradling the stitch that threatened to tear her abdomen in two. James pulled up, panting behind her. There seemed to be no movement on the small, well-lit street to their right and, aside from the steadily moving stream of death on the highway to their left, they looked like they had a clear pass at the camping store that peeked out at them two buildings down.

They picked their way carefully to the edge of the road, the streetlight spotlighting the way in front of them. They moved to the right, skirting the light as though avoiding a fire. They pressed back against the wall and made their way to the back of the store, turning the corner to follow the line of the building, the dry summer grass snapping underfoot. They moved around to the car park that butted up to the camping store; a very well lit, unprotected car park with no cars to provide cover.

'I really hope you can rock-climb,' Sarah whispered over her shoulder, eyes set on the decorative faux waterfall adorning the side of the building. A handy, shoulder-high ledge offered a starting point from which to climb.

James and Sarah moved slowly into the street, the seemingly endless crowd of infected residents continuing to move toward the storm drain, shuffling in eerie sameness. One of the passing horrors crawled toward the others, his back obviously broken from the awkward angle into which it was bent. The creature pulled itself along painfully by its fingertips, dragging useless legs behind him. One awkward pull dragged his ruined torso completely around, so he was facing in their direction.

The siblings froze and Sarah's heart pounded as sightless eyes drifted over their position. They might have passed unnoticed except for the rat that skittered out from behind a rubbish bin beside the store. The minute shudder Sarah wasn't able to hold back was all it took. The crippled zombie released a growl that seemed to be wrenched from the bowels of every horror book and movie she had ever seen.

Sarah started running toward the rock face and could hear James's footsteps close behind her. As they neared the wall, Sarah threw a glance over her shoulder. The creatures closest to them had turned and were moving toward them, several walking quite quickly on undamaged legs. The call of fresh meat rippled outward, drawing them like a magnet toward the camping store. James reached the rocks first and dropped to a knee. Sarah planted a foot on his thigh and launched upwards, landing unsteadily on the narrow ledge. She lowered her hand and grasped James's forearm, wrenching him upward, adrenaline lending her some much-needed strength and muting the pain in her shoulders where the backpack had started to dig into her skin. James crashed into the wall just as the first scrabbling arm groped toward them. Sarah shoved herself backward onto the ornamental rocks. She craned her neck to look up and turned around tightly, reaching up to climb the uncertain holds to the relative safety of the roof. A glance below showed that James was hot on her heels; amazingly the radio was still in his hand. They pulled themselves onto the tin roof and lay panting, exhaustion tearing at their limbs and eyes. Reluctantly, Sarah opened an eye to see James stand up and move toward the middle of the roof.

'Can we stop please? We need to rest. If we get into a fight with them, we won't survive it,' Sarah pleaded.

'I know,' James muttered reluctantly. 'I just want to make sure there's no access to the roof. We don't know what these things are capable of.'

Sarah frowned, but joined him, wavering slightly on weary feet. A quick survey of the roof revealed a raised section of the roof that held a row of windows leading onto the mezzanine floor of the shop. A fire escape enclosed in a locked cage clung to the rear of the building. Assured of the lack of easy access, James and Sarah slid down against the elevated portion of roof onto the corrugated metal, arranging themselves into the least uncomfortable position possible.

'How did you manage to hold onto the radio?' Sarah asked, as sleep pulled at her consciousness.

'It wasn't me,' he huffed. 'I couldn't convince my hand to release it! Believe me, I would have dropped the sucker if I could.' He yawned noisily and they allowed sleep to drag them down.

Sarah woke to a loud buzzing noise, the sharp rumble cutting through the repetitious drone of the hungry creatures below. The sky had begun to lighten, its weak rays illuminating the wrecked scene below. Crawling to the edge, her stiff back complaining from the abuse of the previous night, she assessed the scene. As she had thought, it appeared that the enticement of escape from Geelong's city centre had led to drivers choosing speed over caution. Sarah could see the mangled corpses of at least seven cars creating a gruesome barrier that bisected the highway. The gaps between the hundreds of cars that banked up beyond it were crowded with the meandering trails of the remnants of the city, winding aimlessly in all directions.

The buzzing noise that had woken her grew steadily louder and she raised a hand to shield her eyes, straining to see against the rising sun. A group of black shadows made rapid progress down the street, weaving in and out of cars. Every now and then one steered in close to a shambling figure, striking out and sending it flying. Sarah's eyebrows shot into her hairline in surprise.

A shuffling from behind her nearly pulled a squeal from her throat. She violently choked it back as she spun her head to see James behind her. She pointed out to what became recognisable as seven motorbikes, two of which held tandem riders. Sarah watched carefully as they neared. As they drew closer, Sarah could make out their attire; each of the riders had full-face helmets on, unsuited to the December heat, but good defence against teeth. Two or three held bats that they would occasionally use to belt the walking figures, enough to knock them away if not destroying their heads completely.

Their weapons, however, were not what appeared to hold James's attention. 'Frenzies! See their vests?' he pointed out to Sarah. Each rider sported a design that had been splashed across the evening news frequently—the stylised hornet of the Frenzy biker gang.

Sarah dropped lower to her belly on the roof, unhappily reminded that not all the survivors they came across would be happy to protect them without expecting something in return. The hidden siblings remained still as the swarm of bikes sped past, three of the seven bikes wheeling down the road that they had sprinted across the night before. James silently moved into a crouch, staying low as he moved to the other side of his sister to keep an eye on them as they rode past the rock wall they had climbed up the night before. Sarah stayed where she was, watching as the four bikes that remained at the front created a pied piper effect, leading the rest on a conga line through the cars. She heard a single gunshot from the side and spun quickly to face James. He held up his hand in the shape of a gun and mimed opening a door. The whooping and hollering created discord as the heavy, dull thwacks of the bats met flesh, and occasionally glass, leaving destruction in their wake. Barely ten minutes passed before the four bikes sped into sight once more, laden down with heavy bags. They veered into the crowded street and joined the others, their jeers subsiding into the distance. Sarah gathered her courage again and stood, James following her lead.

'They broke into the side entrance, but we can't use it now. It's secure, but surrounded again.' Sarah turned her attention to the raised part of the roof. The dusty bank of windows that peered onto the upper floor offered little hint as to what waited for them inside.

Sarah was still surprised to see the automatic doors intermittently opening and closing as undefined figures passed within range of the sensors, until she remembered this had all started in the middle of the Boxing Day sales. As far as she could make out, there seemed to be no zombies in the store; however, she could only see about half of the floor from the window where she stood. There were no bars along the window to hinder their passage, but none of them seemed to have a latch that could be jimmied. The second window from the end had, at some point, encountered a projectile, possibly of the winged variety, if the brownish stains that still smeared the sharp edges were anything to go by. The small hole that this left, however, was surrounded by a shattered starburst that Sarah examined closely. She stuck her finger in and wiggled it. The give was negligible, but it was there, and she pulled. Her skin tore and she withdrew her finger quickly with a muffled yell, sticking it in her mouth to soothe the pain.

James gave her a disgusted look and held up the wire cutters. The handle was thin enough to provide leverage without the risk of injury. Sarah gave a 'get on with it' shrug and moved aside. Inserting the handle into the hole he pulled gently, causing the splinter to streak up, and small shards to shower onto the floor below the window. A decent size sliver broke away, landing silently on a pile of tents below and James moved faster, secure in the knowledge that the minuscule noises were not going to expose their position. He glanced down at the floor.

'I think if I lower you down, and you throw some crap in a heap to break my fall we should be right.'

Sarah joined him at the edge, peering down sceptically at the drop.

'Well, better you than me. Grab the para-cord from the front pocket, would you?' Sarah said, turning so James could access the bag on her back. He pulled it out, watching as she painstakingly untied the decorative knot and passed him the ends.

'Are you sure that's strong enough?' James asked, eyeing the thin cord that was now wrapped around his arm. She grabbed the ends and bundled them through the broken window. With one last look at James, she grinned and leaned forward, dropping slowly through to hang her weight from the cord. James grunted under the sudden weight and she glared up at him.

'Arse,' she muttered, startling a laugh out of him. She dropped gingerly to the floor, holding her hand up to catch the radio that he dropped through after her. She pushed a pile of sleeping bags against the wall as he gripped the window and swung himself inside onto the soft pile below.

'… and you're a show off,' she finished.

They took in the shop floor, littered with tents, sleepers and sand huts. In the middle was a wide staircase leading to the main floor, where the front door continued to open and close, stuck in its regular routine. Resting prone on the floor, Sarah could make out a pair of legs in the shoe department and she could hear a shuffling directly below her. The front entrance was directly ahead, the door control switch barely visible to the right of the door behind the counter. The top of the counter sat low enough that a quick jump would get someone over it, and it was high enough to provide a bit of a barrier against sneak attacks while the automatic door was turned over to manual.

As the faster of the two, James raced as quietly as he could down the stairs and leapt to the top of the counter, balancing tentatively on the narrow bench. Sarah saw him struggle to reach the switch, refusing to jump down behind the safety of the counter. As James's fingers closed around the door switch to turn it to manual, Sarah saw the first figure turn, the deep growl reverberating through the store as it moved toward her brother. James remained on his high perch, but turned to the new threat, wielding his metal bar like a baseball bat. It was at the far end of the counter now, a scant two metres away.

Sarah could see another figure closing the gap behind the first, this one wearing the tattered uniform of a store employee. She crept down the stairs, painfully aware that a mere twitch of its head would give the creature a clear view of her position as it moved into the front half of the store toward James. She hefted her bar, her foot touching the carpet at the base of the stairs as James drew close enough to strike. His arm came down in a vicious arc and buried the bar deep in the oncoming skull with a nauseating crunch. Sarah slipped behind the other and swiped upward, the hooked end lodging into the soft skin under the creature's jaw, sticking fast for an awful moment. She wrenched the hook backward and turned green as half his face came with it. Fighting down the rising nausea she brought the bar up again, swiping it forcefully into the side of the head. The spine snapped cleanly, the already compromised throat splitting under the force, sending the head careening into the kayaks lining the wall. Deprived of whatever was keeping the body moving in an awful parody of human motion, the body dropped in a heap like a discarded rag doll.

She could hear the macabre gurgle from the direction where the head had been propelled but ignored it entirely, struggling to maintain her calm facade. She walked over to James, who had swung his legs over the side of the counter and sat slumped on the bench.

'Why didn't you go behind the bench?' Sarah enquired. James waved a hand carelessly behind him and Sarah leaned over the bench, catching sight of a woman's head connected to a sprawled neck and torso; the legs appeared to have been run through a wood chipper and one of her arms ended below the elbow. A remaining eye drifted vaguely upwards and bloodied lips pulled backward in a mockery of a smile revealing blood-stained teeth. She had raised herself up on a ravaged arm and reached up intermittently with eager fingers, losing balance and falling back to the grey carpet beneath her before trying again. Sarah backed away, the gruesome image engraved in her mind. James jumped down beside her without a word. After all the drama they had endured to get here, it felt surreal to Sarah to be standing in a secured building, in what seemed to be relative safety for the first time since she left home the evening before.

Sarah turned a full circle, taking in the store. The second half of the store seemed to be stocked with shelves of camping equipment. Sarah decided to start there, walking to the back of the store, scanning each aisle as she passed. She heard James behind her rifling through the shelves as they passed. She turned to see him handling a complex Leatherman tool.

'Bring a few of them,' Sarah said, before walking toward the back wall, which was covered with suitcases and bags. Her eye caught the red bags of the first-aid kits secured to a post, and she stuffed two of the larger ones in the bottom of a duffle bag. She saw James throw several multi-tools into a bag he had liberated from the pile. She threw a few of the first aid kits over to him. Heading back to the front half of the store, she stopped every now and then to add fire starters and knives, or fishing line and hooks, even finding a portable solar charging kit that folded up neatly into her duffle. Then she focused on the shelf to her left, where an axe sat innocently at waist height. She hefted it up for a closer look, almost dropping it with the surprising weight. It might make for a cleaner defence, but the heaviness would take its toll.

James picked it up and turned it over, tucking it into the bag at his shoulder. 'I'll take it. I can probably do more damage with it than you,' he said, referring pointedly to her lack of musculature.

Sarah pouted. 'You're just jealous because I'm the pretty one,' she shot back.

James laughed and moved further down the same aisle. He paused at the line of generators. 'Should we take one of these? We might need it.'

Sarah shook her head. 'It's likely we'll need to move quickly—these things are far too heavy. We have the solar kit.' She patted her duffle. 'We'll make do.'

They moved away from the generators, leaving the bags near the front counter and walking back through the store. Sarah moved quickly, gathering up a few water reserves, and a couple of torches, batteries and waterproof matches, dividing them equally between the bags. A second radio, fortunately the same model as the one they already had, was picked up from the electronics section. They tossed in pairs of hiking shoes for everyone, dividing them between the bags and put everything in the centre of the main floor, eyeing the collection. Sarah returned to the shelves and retrieved an armful of rope bundles.

'Just in case your almighty ego snaps what little rope we have,' she said sweetly.

James just rolled his eyes.

'We should probably get shelter as well,' she mused, looking up at the mezzanine level.

James scoffed. 'I thought you wanted to be able to move quickly! Have you felt the weight of those things?'

Sarah's face dropped but she brightened quickly and ran upstairs. 'These aren't!' She smiled, holding a packed tarp in hand. 'These and a few sleeping bags and we'll be right,' she said flinging four of the plastic sheets down the stairs. James grabbed a packing strap from the counter and secured them to the bags. Sarah came downstairs, tugging four sleeping bags behind her.

'Is that all they had?' James asked.

'Unless you wanted the Disney one?' she shot back. 'I just grabbed the most expensive ones there—figure you pay for quality, right?'

'Not that you're paying,' he shot back.

'Yeah! Bargain!' She stuffed two sleeping bags into each duffle bag and stood back, looking between the accumulated pile and the mass of goods stacked high throughout the store.

'There's so much that we could use,' she lamented. 'But it's already going to be difficult getting home.'

James nodded and looked beyond the pile to the closed glass doors, eyeing the persistent stream of teeth blocking them from the street beyond. It was obvious that the front door wasn't the way out, and there was no using the window again. They could try the side door that the Frenzy members had used, but the last time they'd seen the road beyond it, the infected mob had been thick.

'What about the back service entry? There has to be something behind the shop?' James asked.

Sarah's face lit up with hope. If the zombies had crowded around the front doors because of the movement and sound they had seen, the back door might still be clear. Sarah ran back to the shelves and picked up a cheap rechargeable AM/FM radio. She put it against the front door and turned it on, cranking the volume up to its loudest. The emergency broadcast nearly shook the doors where the crowds had started to gather, attracted to the noise. She levelled a scowl at the milling horde pulling the gore-spattered fire tool from her backpack before picking up one of the bags. Slowly, they headed to the back, pushing open the 'staff only' door.

Walking through into a small, office-like space, desks littered with now useless papers Sarah felt like an intruder. Scribbled post-it notes reminded employees of meetings that would not be held and made pithy comments that would go unappreciated. They walked through the double doors into a warehouse filled with towering boxes, waiting for shoppers that would never come. Sarah turned her attention to locating the door that would hopefully lead to a clear outdoors.

James put his bag down and ran over to a desk nestled in the corner behind them. When he returned, he had ten rolls of gaffer tape in his arms. 'Good for everything,' he smirked, piling them into the bag at his feet.

They stood in front of a closed door with a green exit sign illuminated above it. Sarah twisted the deadlock that was keeping the door secure and pushed it open, letting the December heat invade the cool dark of the warehouse.

# Chapter Six

Seth lay across the shabby couch, trying unsuccessfully to convince his body to ignore the adrenaline rush and rest. Through half slit eyelids, he could see Rebecca where she sat with her hands resting on her knees, back pushed into a corner of the couch. She stared blankly at the calendar tacked to the wall; a blonde in a swimsuit draped over a yellow sports car looked coyly back at the room. A big black line bisected the square containing the number 23. She uncurled herself from the couch and walked over to the calendar, crossing out the public holiday dates and then blacking out the twenty-six box entirely, so no white could be seen.

'Black box for a black day,' she said morosely.

'Bit dark don't you think? At least your family is most likely intact,' Seth said lightly, giving up on his fight for sleep.

She winced, remembering that he had lost his sister, but she didn't turn to face him. 'It seemed fitting. Someone has to mark it.' She twisted the black texta in her fingers and faced him. 'What now?' she asked, happy to rely on someone else for a while.

'Well, you seem set on getting to your family, and I'm stuck here for the time being,' he stated bluntly. He walked to the desk in the small office and pulled the novelty map off the wall, ripping the corners slightly. He weighted it down with a cup and a stapler on the floor between them and plucked the texta from Rebecca's fidgeting fingers. He traced a thick circle around the tyre factory and tapped it absentmindedly. A second circle surrounded the hospital and he recapped the texta. He rested the base on the white lines that protruded out into the blue of the bay, marking the large marina that was nestled between several restaurants directly below the hospital. Another circle was drawn around that. Seth sat back on his heels and eyed the map. Rebecca looked at him, confusion wrinkling the skin around her eyes.

'Care to share?' she asked. He took a moment to his gather his thoughts.

'This … thing hit in the middle of Boxing Day, arguably the busiest time of the year. Every shop in here,' he tapped the shaded area that marked off the CBD, 'would have been completely full of people.' He paused, watching as Rebecca slowly drew the same conclusions.

'We can't go through the city?' she asked.

Seth nodded. 'We also have to keep in mind that the first instinct of every human is to take sick and injured people *to* the hospital.' He spoke softly, not wanting to state the brutal facts before she could see them for herself.

Her stubborn expression implied that she did, indeed, understand where he had been headed and did not appreciate the warning at all. He held his hands up.

'Look, there may be an option here,' he pointed to the circled marina. 'If we can get here, it's a straight line up to the hospital and it bypasses the majority of the city. We can work our way along the waterfront till we get there. Hopefully the numbers will be concentrated away from the waterfront.'

'What about the crowds *on* the waterfront?' Rebecca asked. 'Between Cunningham Pier and the marina is a huge tourist spot, not to mention the dozens of shops and restaurants, and the hotel.'

'It's still less than what will certainly be in the city, and hopefully when we get closer, we'll see what we have to work with.' Seth was reasonably sure that there would be something he could use to take them out into the bay a short distance if necessary. He knew that between them there was a severe lack of boating knowledge, but if they stayed within sight of land they could avoid too many problems.

Rebecca was silent as her eyes drifted over the map, her gaze locking on the train station, the greyish block at the end of the road they were on.

'There's a police station at the end of this road, just in front of the train station,' she mused aloud. 'I know you have that baton thing …'

'Asp,' he interrupted.

Rebecca continued as though he hadn't said a word. '… but at the moment I have nothing suitable.'

'You looked pretty comfortable with that tyre iron,' Seth scoffed.

She glared at him, although the slight creases around her eyes gave away her amusement. 'And yet you were able to take that away with very little effort,' she reminded him. 'It's unwieldy, it has no grip, and won't be much use in the long term.' She ticked off the points on her fingers as she made them.

'Right, got it—we need weapons.' Another circle marred the surface of the map. 'With all the riots in the city, they probably sent out the majority of the force. There would only be a skeleton crew left at best, if they survived at all,' Seth said sombrely. 'That will take us very close to the city.' His eyes followed the path that led them to the police station. 'Are you sure you can do this?'

Rebecca said nothing, rolling to her feet and stretching. Now that a plan had been voiced, the air was tense and urgent. Together, they moved to the main door that looked out onto the empty car park at the front entrance. Nothing moved; no cars lined the black street. Seth could feel his neck tense as adrenaline coursed through his body. He forced himself to breathe deeply and focus before unlocking the door and stepping out into the hot summer morning.

A high concrete wall hedged the property on the city side, providing cover while obstructing the view of the car park from the street. He cautiously looked around the corner, Rebecca behind him, pressed firmly against the wall.

'It looks clear, but there's no way of knowing what's down the side streets,' he muttered. 'Stay here till I tell you otherwise.'

She nodded, and he slipped out from the cover of the wall, walking slowly toward the nearest corner. He visually cleared the street with a glance before crossing and waving Rebecca forward.

They advanced slowly, making gradual headway down the street. There were four blocks between them and the traffic lights that indicated the position of the police station, the artistic spears of the outer fence barely visible from the corner they were huddled behind. They looked out into a five-way intersection that spider-webbed across the empty road. Rebecca had almost forgotten about the steady hum that had reverberated through the air the previous day, but the further they walked, the louder it grew, until it mutated into a constant drone that rattled their teeth.

'What is that?' she asked softly.

Seth clenched his hands into fists, one gripping the heavy asp. He pressed a finger to his lips, indicating the need for silence, and pointed slowly around the corner.

Following his finger, Rebecca craned around Seth before snapping her head back behind the wall, biting her lip to suppress the scream that she desperately wanted to release, and closing her eyes tight. The street was a large two-lane road with centre parking, which stretched the width to about three lanes across. The lane ran parallel to the waterfront, a block away from the bay, and made up one side of the CBD border. Although her glance down the street had taken barely a second, what she had seen was burned behind her eyelids. The entirety of the street was crawling with zombies, the road completely obscured from view by the seething swarm.

'What now?' she mouthed.

Seth had been looking around frantically, searching for a way across that would keep them from being spotted, but coming up completely dry of ideas. Suddenly Rebecca yanked on his shirt-sleeve, drawing his attention.

'We might not make it past them unseen, but what if we only have to make it two streets? They don't run … they barely walk!'

Seth looked confused so she snatched the map from his back pocket, opening it just enough to show their position and the police station. The growling buzz burned at their ears, seeming to grow in intensity. She stabbed a finger at the train station.

'There's a tunnel here. It runs under the police station and comes out here,' she jabbed again, this time at a patch of green two streets away from where they crouched.

Seth looked up, measuring the distance that separated them, and back down the crowded street. His eyes widened slightly as he whipped his head back around.

'Given that they seem to have decided to head this way, we'll go with that. You know where the tunnel is, so you go first. I'll be right behind.'

Rebecca tensed, gathering her legs beneath her.

'Go,' he hissed, and she shot off across the road, hearing the now clearly identifiable growls change into vicious snarls as they ran into view. She flew across the baking cement, eyes fixed on the raised cracked footpath that she knew was atop the hidden tunnel. Seth checked his own steps as she veered sharply to the left, vaulting the chain link fence effortlessly before falling down the steep mossy sides that lined the mouth of the tunnel. Seth's weight barrelled into her from behind, shoving her to the ground with a grunt. Wordlessly, he scrambled back to his feet, grasping her hand in his and yanking her to her feet. They ran further into the cool dark of the cavernous opening as a steady rolling snarl passed overhead. Limping footsteps and the constant thump of flesh and bone reverberated in the hollow tube. They crouched beside the cold walls until Rebecca began to slide further into the shadows, Seth keeping pace, mimicking her moves.

It felt like hours later when the noise finally gave way to relative silence. Only the odd slide was heard overhead, the snarls moving into the background once more. Rebecca looked to Seth, releasing a shaky laugh, and he offered a small smile in return, almost invisible in the muted light.

Seth looked at their surroundings, pulling out a small set of keys and turning the weak beam of a cheap keyring torch onto the ancient walls and floor. He had kept count of his steps as they buried deeper into the tunnel and guessed they were just about under the police station. The ceiling offered no grate access or manholes, arching over uninterrupted to meet the floor again. He ran a finger across the seam of the bricks, barely held together by the aged mortar. Seth smiled. Depending on where they managed to break through at the surface, they should have little problem with breaking through the brick above. He held his hand out to Rebecca.

'Pass the tyre iron, please?' She pressed the weighty bar into his hand and he dug the sharp bevelled edge into the crumbling mortar and shoved, coughing and blinking at the flurry of dust and cement that showered onto his upturned face. He turned to face her, wiping the detritus from his eyes. 'We should be able to dig through this part, but I'll need your help though.'

She nodded and sat down. 'There's only one tool and you have possession of that at the moment,' she pointed out. 'Let me know when you need a break.' She settled back against the wall and closed her eyes with a grin. Seth scowled, turning to the bricks and chipping away steadily.

They made several swaps between them, gradually widening

the hole above them to about a metre in diameter. The bricks had posed no problems and were quickly piled up in a heap along the wall. The layer of dirt underneath the bricks had been a little surprising but was easily passable. They stopped to catch their breath, the hole showing thick oak boards above them.

Rebecca reached up, surprised. 'I thought it would have been concrete?'

'Depends on the age of the building. Geelong is still an old city and the new police station is just a modified veneer holding an old shell together. They probably left the foundations for convenience.' His voice sounded strained and Rebecca knew hers did too. The heavy labour and dusty air combined with weary muscles and empty bellies did not make for happy workers.

She picked up the tyre iron.

'We need to take a break,' he stated firmly. Rebecca shook her head, but Seth shot her a sharp look. 'It's going to be a lot of work getting past that, *if* we can get past it. We need to eat, and rest. We're no good to anyone like this, least of all ourselves,' he reasoned, knowing that she wouldn't be able to keep her family safe if she were exhausted when she found them. Seth continued: 'I need water, and breakfast. You said this tunnel used to be a railway tunnel?'

Rebecca nodded, although her hand still rested on the iron, eager to work on and get to her family. Seth pressed his point home, appealing to the common sense that had been overtaken by her protective side.

'So there has to be an end at the railway station, and I'm sure, like every good railway station, there's a cafeteria somewhere inside. We can stop for an hour and regroup so you're not too tired to be any use to your family.'

Rebecca grimaced. 'Cafeteria may be stretching it a little,' she said grudgingly. 'More like a kiosk.'

'Food is food,' he shrugged, retrieving the tyre iron from the ground and walking further into the gloomy tunnel.

Seth found it first, the subtle shift of air marking the shadowed end of the tunnel. He reached out his hand to rest on the heavy wooden door in front of him, the thin light from the key chain danced along the wood, searching out the shiny deadlock securing the door tightly within its frame. Seth wedged the chipped bevelled edge of the iron between the seam of the door and the hinge, wrenching backward. Hearing a faint whine of protest from the rusting hinges, he anchored one foot on the wall beside the door and strained backward again. This time, the screech of nails parting from wood echoed loudly in the tunnel. He stopped for a moment, ears straining for any indication that they had been heard. A heavy silence hummed back at him. He sighed in relief, pulling the tyre iron out of the narrow gap between door and doorpost, and kicking the door sharply, sending it careening inwards, held on at one side by the shiny new deadbolt. He climbed into the room and watched as Rebecca climbed over the fallen wood to join him.

They found themselves in what appeared to be a storage room. Grey filing cabinets lined the room like gravestones around the stairs that formed the centrepiece to the room. The door at the top looked dark and solid; Seth doubted it would give as easily as the first door. He climbed the stairs slowly, testing each step individually for squeaks or groans that might give them away. He pushed the door open, just enough to look into the room beyond, before beckoning for Rebecca to join him.

'It opens into the room behind the ticket counter. There are five employees in there. Can't see if they're infected or not, but there are about ten infected people beyond that in the waiting area.'

'There are survivors?' she asked excitedly. 'That's fantastic!'

'We barely made it this far with only two of us, and now you want to add five frightened sheep to the mix?' The thought of dragging more people into this farcical rescue effort weighed heavily in his stomach.

Rebecca frowned. 'Those "sheep" are people,' she spat back. 'What about the police station?'

Seth arched an eyebrow, clearly questioning the effect of sleep deprivation and stress on her cognitive skills.

She grunted in frustration. 'They can help break through the floor. You said yourself that it would be hard work—they can help! Oh, and tools … they would have better tools for maintenance in the rail yard!' She tripped over her tongue as she tried to make her case. 'Plus, they could know of other tunnels connected to the railway yard. They might come in handy.'

Seth bowed his head in frustrated resignation. 'I'm *not* playing babysitter,' he growled, before rapping on the solid door, warning the inhabitants of their presence. A startled, half-smothered scream came from the room in response.

'Who's there?' The shaky voice was undeniably female with an alto tone that hinted at her age, one who had perhaps taken the role of spokesperson.

'My name is Seth. I'm here with one other person. Her name is Rebecca.' He pitched his voice as though speaking to a frightened child. 'We're not infected, we just want to talk. Can we come in?' There was a flurry of whispers barely discernible through the thick wood as the occupants debated whether to trust the faceless voice. The first voice returned, slightly stronger this time.

'Okay, but slowly. Hands first, we're armed!' she stated brusquely.

Seth nudged the door open, pushing his hands into the narrow gap and edging it open the rest of the way with his hip. He smothered a grin as he caught sight of their 'weapons'. He was fairly sure a stapler wouldn't offer up too much of a fight, either against them or the zombies outside, even if the wielder had spectacular aim.

The ruler was not much better, although the chair leg might at least offer a weak defence at first.

Rebecca stepped up next to Seth, hands raised. Nobody moved toward them to take their weapons, speaking clearly of their lack of preparation for such a situation. Seth was glad he would not have to prevent them from removing his weapon, secured as it was in his back pocket.

The spokesperson was a neatly dressed lady in a rail worker's uniform, who looked to be in her mid-forties. She crouched against a chair, remaining below the level of the bench, her stocking-clad legs bent under her, greying hair pulled back into a messy bun at the nape of her neck. A nametag identified her as Karen and she looked beyond tired, her makeup wilting in the stuffy room. She held the chair leg across her lap and despite her outwardly calm appearance her fingers were white where they gripped the shaft in a stranglehold. The brownish-red stains on the wood suggested it had recently been used. All of them stayed low, either seated or crouched on the floor, out of sight of what was beyond the glass wall of the service desk.

'Karen? I'm Seth.' He smiled in what he hoped was a reassuring manner. 'This is Rebecca.' He nodded in her direction, not taking his eyes from Karen's.

The older woman nodded unsmilingly and gestured to the four people behind her. 'Peter, Luke, Sue and Sam,' she said, by way of an introduction. Peter and Luke were identical, their deep green eyes mirroring each other under their dark brown hair. Luke seemed to have positioned himself slightly in front of his brother, possibly hinting at the age order of the two. Sam towered over them even in their crouched positions. Seth was impressed; despite Sam's low position, he looked ready to spring into action. His grey eyes were shaded by straight black hair, lanky legs drawn up slightly as he leaned against the far wall. Sue had pulled her long legs up tight, white hair draped over knees that hid her face, compressing herself into the smallest possible ball. A dragonfly tattoo wrapped around her ankle, giving her a delicate feel that instantly put her in the liability list Seth was writing in his head, Seth nodded to each in turn, the smile not wavering on his face.

'Have you all been here since yesterday?' he asked.

Luke spoke up, his voice strained from the heightened stress, his green eyes wide in his tanned face.

'Yeah. It wasn't this bad then. There was only one at first … Looked like he was sick, all hunched over and moaning …' His voice trailed off as he recalled the events, eyes drifting as the movie replayed in front of his eyes. 'He ate him … Tore his face off with his teeth … Oh God … I thought it was a sick joke!' Luke's retelling picked up speed, words tangling into a barely decipherable garble. 'We called security. Johnny tried to stop him! Tackled him to the ground and all! Nothing worked!' Here his voice cracked, his eyes locked with Seth's. 'We panicked! Sealed off the security window and hid in here.' Shame trickled into his words and he looked away, focusing on the dirty carpet at his feet. 'They tore into everyone!'

Sue's small voice broke into the stillness; her fingers played with the ends of her blonde hair as she spoke. 'We couldn't do anything!' Somehow her voice managed to sound both defensive and broken as she jumped to defend their actions. 'They came too quick. If we had opened the door, no one would have made it.'

Seth turned to Karen as weariness weighed his aching arms down. Karen watched him warily but made no move to stop him.

'You were right,' he said gently, rubbing his neck to get the feeling back. 'They're too much, too …'

'Unnatural,' Rebecca murmured.

Karen seemed to relax at the lack of judgement, her reaction allowing the others to uncurl a little.

'How bad is it out there?' Karen asked hesitantly, unsure if she really wanted to hear the answer.

Seth hesitated, eyes flicking over the teenagers before shaking his head. 'With the crowds in the city for the sales, there would have been a lot of panic. We passed the freeway on the way here. It looks like a car park. I can't even guess how many might have survived.' He hesitated, debating the wisdom of offering what might turn out to be a false dream. 'I think that refugee camps have been set up in the city.'

'They have!' Rebecca jumped in, eager to share what she knew. 'The emergency warning said they were moving people to the old gaol.'

A loud sob broke from Sue and her pale face lowered to her knees. Peter, who was closest, placed an arm around her shoulder.

Karen explained: 'Luke and Peter were able to call out and talk to their sister. She's all that's left of their family. She's in the gaol.' Karen paused before continuing. 'Sue and Sam couldn't reach their families, though Sam is from Tasmania, so we're hoping that the infection hasn't reached there. The mobiles stopped working fairly soon after that.'

It was apparent from what Karen omitted that she, too, was unable to contact family, but hadn't wanted to broach the subject.

'We would have used the radio to call for help but unfortunately it's out there.' Karen's gaze drifted to the side door that led beyond the safety glass. They could still hear the low growls from the larger room and see the shadowy forms move past the smeared glass. A closer examination showed that the door didn't actually open directly onto the main floor, but into an area that was separated entirely from the main floor by a solid, waist-high desk.

Seth could barely make out the oversized instrument panel that hunkered below the top of the desk. A whooshing noise had every head whipping around to look at the door. One of the creatures inside the door had wandered within the range of detection and sent the automated doors sliding open noisily. Seth could see that the attention of some of the closer unfortunates had been sharp enough to register the change and had started a painful step-drag in their direction, hampered by a broken leg.

'How do you shut the doors?' Seth asked urgently.

Luke pointed a finger toward the radio. 'There's a main switch beside the radio that controls all the automatic external doors,' he said.

'While I'm securing the doors, see if you can find something heavier than a stapler for a weapon.' Seth pointedly ignored the flush that crept across Karen's cheeks as he walked in a low crouch out the door.

He was back quickly. The switch had been easy to find and deactivate. As he came back in, he noted the boys had started turning the desks inside out, looking for weapons.

'I counted ten of them out there, something we can work with, but just do what you can … and don't get bitten. How are we going with weapons?'

Sam raised his head from the draw he was currently buried in. 'Would this help?' A roll of material tape hung from his finger.

Seth frowned. 'We're not looking for hostages,' he said.

Sam rolled his eyes before pulling at the edge and wrapping it around his arm, covering the skin from wrist to elbow.

'Have you tried to bite through one of these? Might not stop a huge crowd, but one or two? Could stop their bite enough to get away.' He shrugged before wrapping his other arm as well as his lower legs.

Seth let out a laugh. The boy looked ridiculous, but if it worked … He snatched the roll when Sam had finished with it, copying the boy's actions and then passing the roll to Rebecca.

'We need to clear the room and get to the kiosk. I doubt anyone else has eaten since this started. Once that's done, we'll have a look at the radio. Maybe we can get hold of someone in the city, get a better idea of what's happening.'

Sue's thin voice piped up once again. 'Clear the room, how?' She had unfurled from her ball and now crouched near the boys.

Seth smiled in a decidedly unfriendly manner. 'There's ten of them and seven of us. That's only one or two each with what I have in mind. We stand a better chance at taking them out quickly in a surprise attack while they're distracted. We need to clear them out though. The desk is low enough that we might get lucky and they'll fall over it.'

The boys seemed to perk up at the thought of evening the score a little, although Seth would've bet his pension that the closest any of them had come to violence in the past was through video games. Karen and Sue, on the other hand, were not happy. Karen was subtle about expressing her disapproval, jaw clenching, the muscles around her eyes twitching as she looked between the boys and the creatures behind the window. Sue unsurprisingly took the verbal route.

'I can barely kill a spider and you want me to brain those things?' The disgust at the idea was clear in her voice.

Rebecca stood up, radiating a controlled fury as she stalked over to the girl. 'I left my daughter with my husband's parents to make *damn* sure that my whole family is safe, and I intend to make it back to her. If you stand between me and that goal, know that I will do whatever it takes to make it back to her.' She left the threat hanging, allowing Sue to draw her own conclusions. Her hand clenched around the bar that had remained in her hand since they walked into the room. The ice that coated Rebecca's words stunned Sue into silence.

Sue looked desperately to the others in the room for support but found nothing except frowns that seemed to be directed at her. She stalked over to the small pile of scavenged weapons the boys had gathered, picking up a slender pipe they had removed from an old heater.

'Go team,' she spat out, returning to her corner.

The boys paid little attention to the sulking girl, turning their chosen weapons over in their hands. Luke held a large knife pilfered from the tiny kitchenette at the back of the room; Peter was swinging another snapped-off chair leg from side-to-side as he became accustomed to the weight. Sam had found a heavy metal torch in one of the desks at the back of the room, and was absent-mindedly flicking it on and off. The beam danced off the security glass, illuminating the snarling face of a zombie pressed against the glass. The ghastly figure seemed transfixed by the flashing light, its milky eyes not wavering from the brightness.

Seth frowned, watching the odd behaviour, before flicking the light switch on, bathing the room in light and causing everyone to wince. The sudden change drew the attention of the other creatures that continued to move aimlessly beyond the glass. As one they turned, some less gracefully than others, and stumbled their way toward the brightly lit wall.

'They seem to be focused on the light,' Seth muttered, turning to Karen. 'If you can keep their focus here, we can take them out from behind.' As he spoke, he moved toward the door with the boys and Rebecca trailing behind.

Karen started banging at the window as the creatures' attention began to split between them and the new movement. Sue looked uncooperative until a pointed look from Rebecca had her scrambling to join Karen. The distraction worked as Seth had hoped it would.

While the small crowd of malodorous creatures were pawing fruitlessly at the thick glass, Seth led his group in a wide arc, keeping them low so as not to draw attention prematurely. Silently, they climbed under the hinged part of the desk, moving behind the distracted creatures. Seth flicked his asp out, the soft *schwick* barely registering in his ears, although it was loud enough to gain the attention of what had once been a young man in thongs and board shorts, his rib cage now partially exposed under a mess of tissue. The creature's head turned stiffly, shoulders and body twisting awkwardly as it looked at them. It opened its mouth as if to snarl but Seth shut it up swiftly, whipping the baton down hard. An audible crack signalled the destruction of the bone beneath and it crumpled to the ground like a discarded toy.

Rebecca dispatched a young woman in a yellow dress, the momentum tearing the bar from her hand. She didn't stop to witness the graceless fall before she was spinning a solid kick into the sternum of an elderly man behind her. His leg was clearly broken, brittle white bone stabbing through torn skin. He fell onto the tall back of the bench behind him, his aged spine snapping sharply as he folded onto himself, wrapped around the wooden slats. Rebecca grimaced in disgust as he attempted to pull himself off the chair. She hefted up a heavy pole from the floor beside her, still tethered by a braided rope, and slammed the heavy base down on the old man's skull.

Luke, Peter and Sam had thrown themselves into the shuffling crowd, swinging and hacking at the not quite dead creatures. Seth looked around to see the boys panting hard, each covered in spatters of blood and gore. Luke seemed to have copped the worst of it; he twitched uncomfortably, tugging at the now red shirt where it clung to his chest.

'It never seemed this messy on the telly,' he quipped. Sam and Peter joined his chuckles, coaxing a grin from Seth and Karen.

Sue merely sneered at the group. 'Really?' she snarked. The smiles began to wilt a little and Karen smacked a heavy hand across the back of Sue's head.

'Show a little respect to the people who just saved your life,' she snapped at her. Sue just glared sullenly at the ground, the red that crept up her neck closely matching the colour of Luke's shirt.

It was Peter who brought them back to the issue at hand, his stomach growling in a parody of the beasts they had just felled.

Seth smiled and crossed to the counter that was still stocked with food. 'Who's hungry then?' he asked.

Sue's red faced turned slightly green while the others just lined up in front of the kiosk.

Seth pointed to the toilets. 'Wash your hands thoroughly first. I don't want to have to deal with an infection via stupidity.' He moved to clean his own hands at the sink.

Karen checked each of them carefully as they returned to the counter, waiting as Seth pulled the fruit and pastries from the counter and handed them out.

'It's not gourmet, but it's all I'm making,' he said as he passed the food over the counter. Even cold, the snacks made a filling meal and sent the group into a post meal lethargy they were unable to fight. Seth steered them all back to the cleaner's office area and directed them to get rest while they could. No one argued.

Seth watched as the others settled down to rest, looking for something to stave of his own exhaustion. His eyes fell on the radio in the next room. Walking through to the panel, he turned it on, twisting the dial to move past the static feed.

'... has declared a state of emergency in the southern states. People are advised to remain in their homes or move to designated safe areas in their cities if remaining at home is impossible. The defence force has been mobilised to contain this threat. Residents are asked not to put themselves at risk by acting on their own. If you are unable to receive the emergency message on your mobile device, a list of local refugee areas will follow.'

The voice stopped and another monotone recording began.

'The region of *Geelong* has the following safe areas … *Old Geelong Gaol* …'

After the list was complete, the first voice came on once more.

'The Prime Minister has declared a state of emergency in the southern states …'

Seth flicked the radio off and mixed up a cold coffee in the kitchen, settling in for a long wait.

Meanwhile, miles away, Melbourne had always been a busy city, happy to have any excuse for a fantastic spectacle, wowing the multitudes that pounded its streets. Boxing Day was no exception, but this time its grand parade of tens of thousands had turned against it.

# Chapter Seven

Hours after her lighthearted conversation with Sarah, Jen found herself huddled in the cellar of the Royal Melbourne Hospital, cursing the crowds that had brought the virus to the city's door. They had worked non-stop, moving the stable patients into the more secure concrete service rooms below the hospital, before shutting the entrances down completely. The intensive care patients had been left with a skeleton staff, with most of the generator power diverted to the ward after a collision between tram and traffic had brought down the power lines. They had been fortunate in having the advanced warning from the authorities. As brief as it was, it was enough to enable them to make an identification chart to check against the possible infected, and they had made the decision to turn away any patient that matched the criteria, although some had still managed to secure a place behind the solid walls before the doors were shut. Now, thousands of patients and family members were crowded into the reinforced bunkers under the hospital.

Jen was quietly proud of what they had managed to pull together in the past three days. Storerooms, cellars and part of the expansive tunnels that weaved under the city streets had been turned into a tent city, families and patients joining the homeless on the damp concrete as they fought for space. The unusual mix had not been without its problems; several people had complained about the proximity of 'questionable types', insisting their children and families be separated from the unwashed tunnel residents who spoke to the voices in their heads and scared the younger refugees with their bizarre behaviour. Fights had been broken up as tensions ran high and supplies were strictly rationed. The unrest had been the reason behind the formation of the peacekeepers on the second day. People with enforcement backgrounds—a few military personnel but mostly policemen and security guards—had pulled together and worked in rotations to maintain the building's security upstairs, as well as showing a strong presence downstairs. The hospital's nursing staff had sectioned off several rooms, enlisting the help of the maintenance force to relocate beds from the wards to the lower levels. They had quietly separated those who were identified to have mental health issues and needed additional care into the smaller of the two service rooms. The medical staff organised their own rosters to provide a scant cover throughout the underground city. Most of the refugees had jobs too. They used their skills where they could to make the areas liveable, although many just huddled miserably in the heavy shadows with no distraction to keep the dark thoughts away.

The passages in which they were hiding connected three major hospitals and a large university, allowing easy access to each. Between these, they had split their resources, moving all the food and water they found to the Royal Melbourne Hospital, putting their huge kitchens and the large generator to use and feeding the thousands of dependants now sleeping it its bowels. The children's hospital became the storage for medical supplies and whatever weapons they could scavenge; it had been sealed up like a vault, only accessible to staff who were identified by their photo ID, which was enforced by the receptionists enlisted into guard duty from each of the hospitals. The Royal Women's Hospital had been turned into the only official outside access and communications centre. They had brought in the CB radios from the ambulances in the bay and several paramedics now took turns to cover the airwaves, gleaning any information they could.

The engineers and tradespeople who had found refuge in the hospital had welded metal bed frames to the doors and windows of the entrances, shutting them off completely from the streets above. The web of tunnels that ran from the hub to almost every area in the city were mostly marked as unsafe, the wooden supports in some of the tunnels dating back to World War Two.

Jen took supplies up to the paramedics in the communications centre. She passed a coffee to Daniel, a paramedic she had worked with on several occasions before the world went to hell.

'Quiet day today?' she asked, pulling out the chair next to him. He nodded as he slowly turned the dial, face scrunched up in concentration. They had grown closer, thrust together as they were in the confined space under the hospital, and she was grateful for the close companionship they had developed. She jumped as one of the radios squawked to life under his moving fingers.

'… Geelong, it will cause enough damage cauterise the source. Maybe cause enough confusion that it's buried completely.'

They all froze at the unexpected voice that hissed from the black speakers. Daniel moved to grab the mouthpiece connected to the radio.

'Wait one minute, please?' Jen begged, resting a hand over the radio.

He paused.

'Will it be big enough?' A lower voice responded to the first.

'It should take out most of the city.'

'What about the refugee camp?'

'We have our orders. How many do you truly think have survived this long? We're just waiting for the final go ahead.'

'Stand by, let's make sure our boys are clear.'

Jen turned pale. 'They're going to blow up Geelong,' she said. 'Oh God, Sarah!' She gripped the desk for support, feeling her legs weaken. 'Have you made contact with anyone from Geelong?' she begged. Daniel flipped through a book at his arm.

'We have two—Sarina and Joe. No Sarah, sorry.' He picked up the hand piece to the next radio, tuning into a channel written in the book. A tired female voice came though the speakers.

'Daniel? Is everything okay?'

'It's all good here, Sass. I just needed to give you a heads up on a situation headed your way.'

'To Geelong? No we've moved on. We're about to make our way out to Tasmania now. We found a pilot willing to take us across for food rations.'

'You gave him everything?' he asked, concerned.

'We kept a little aside, but pretty much, yeah.'

'It's good that you're going, for whatever price—just be careful.'

'Roger that.' The woman sighed. 'This is really our only option. There are awful rumours about the refugee camps here. We don't want to find out if they're true.'

They kept their sign-offs short and Daniel dialled into another channel.

'Joe?' he queried into the mouthpiece. Nobody responded. Daniel tried again. 'Joe?' He looked at Jen, who fidgeted anxiously at the front of the desk. 'He may have had to step away. I'll try again in five minutes.'

The radio crackled to life, startling them both.

'That you, Dan?' The gruff voice sounded stressed.

'It's me, how are your lot holding up?'

'We're coping. A few of us are missing, gone into the city. We're waiting for word before we do anything else.'

Daniel frowned. 'I don't know how to say this then. We've had word of a pretty big problem headed your way.'

'A big problem?' Jen could hear Joe's thick sarcasm over the airwaves.

'Bigger,' Daniel insisted. 'It sounds like there may be someone trying to take Geelong off the map completely.' There was a heavy silence over the airwaves, only the quiet hiss of white noise in the hospital reception area.

'What exactly are we talking about here?' Joe had lowered his voice so as not to spook the others in the house with him.

'There has been talk of someone planning to blow up the city. It sounds like their attempt at managing the situation as well as destroying any evidence.'

'Evidence? Evidence of what?' Joe hissed down the line.

Jen saw a muscle jump in Daniel's jaw.

'Honestly? Not a clue. Maybe this is the group responsible for this fuck up.' He hated to say that much, aware that others could be listening in the same way he had discovered the information. Fortunately Joe seemed to have come to the same realisation.

'How much time do we have? Where exactly is the focal point?' Joe asked quietly.

'Uncertain at this point. It sounds big enough that anyone within a ten k radius should think about going to see the countryside. Stay on this channel and we'll give you details as we get them.'

'Understood.' Daniel looked like he was about to sign off.

'Wait!' Jen interrupted frantically. 'Is there a Sarah in your group?'

'Not that I know, but I'm fairly new to this group.' Joe sounded reluctant to part with even that much information.

'Black hair? Blue eyes?' She half expected her query to be brushed aside but pressed on, anxious to know if her friend was still safe.

'Like I said, I don't know.'

Jen sighed in despondency; she slumped into a hard chair in the waiting room, leaving Daniel and Joe to sign off.

# Chapter Eight

Steel walls rose high over the small service entrance to the camping store. A roller door separated the area from the street beyond, stretching up to the roofline of the building. The only other access was the door set into the corrugated iron, the echo of growls reverberating through the thin metal and into the small concrete yard. Sarah and James could just hear the monotone voice of the emergency message from the radio they had turned up loud by the front door. Walking softly, James moved over to the small door and peeked through the narrow crack. He was back just as quickly, eyes wide and breath quick.

'There must be hundreds of them out there!' he gasped out. 'Not all of them were pulled to the front; heaps of them are on the street pressed right up against the walls! We can't get out that way.'

Sarah turned in a full circle, taking in the courtyard properly. It was pretty bare, with a dozen pallets stacked against the wall to the right and a small forklift parked beside them. She drummed her fingers thoughtfully against the strap of her backpack before walking over to the forklift. Slipping the bag off, she dropped it beside James, and climbed up into the small vehicle, sliding into the bouncy seat. The key was still slotted in the ignition and a piercing beep speared through their skulls as she turned it.

The machine lurched forward and stalled and they could hear the sudden swell in the growling behind the tin wall. The iron seemed to screech and pulse inwards, bowing under the weight pressed in behind them. Eyeing the strained hinges, Sarah frantically turned the key again, coaxing the engine into life and fumbling with the levers at her knee. A hesitant pull at the nearest lever had the twin forks jerking lower. She pushed it up, raising it a centimetre above the pavement and shifting it into first gear, inching the forklift forward at a snail's pace across the yard until it butted against the far wall. James stood still beside the bags, watching her in confusion. She swung down out of the seat and ran back to him, slinging one of the bags over her bandaged arm. She beckoned him forward, not wanting to speak and possibly further agitate the creatures seeking a way in.

'I got us a ride,' she whispered. 'Grab the bag.'

Although his posture still radiated apprehension, James pulled the last bags over to the forklift. 'Now what? I know you're not planning to drive through them. We'd be safer on a skateboard.' Though he kept his tone light, Sarah could hear the hint of panic.

She rolled her eyes and rested her bag on one of the long tines that nudged against the wall.

'Oh I don't know,' she drawled. 'Seems like a fun ride. Shall we see how many we can skewer on the way?' She rolled her eyes and pointed a finger skyward. 'We're going up.'

Comprehension washed over James's face, which was then replaced with tangible relief and he, too, rested his load on the thick bar. Sarah opened her bag, pulling out the gaffer tape and securing the bags onto the tine.

A metallic screech turned their heads to the roller door. Their eyes widened in horror as the edges bowing inwards with the heavy weight of the mass behind them now parted wide enough that hands could fit through into the courtyard. The zombies were happily demonstrating the fact, their greedy fingers grasping toward the promise of a meal that was, for now, still out of reach.

'Okay, let's go!' James jumped onto the empty tine, holding

on tightly as Sarah fumbled with the levers once more. A firm pull of the lever had the fork and its contents jerking skywards. Her attention was divided between the complicated controls and the bowing door, so much so that she didn't realise that the forklift had reached its maximum height. James was now teetering precariously just above the roofline. The sudden halting jerk of the machine tore a surprised gasp from her throat. A screeching whine from the stressed door had her scrambling from her seat and climbing with surprising grace up the side of the forklift, clambering to where the bags dropped between tape and tine. Her fingers tore at the gaffer tape still holding the bags in place. She tossed her backpack on top of the others, jumping across to the roof after it. The haunting squeal of tearing metal gave way to an echoing crash as the door surrendered to the mass behind it, ripping up from the ground, now secured only by the crossbar above. It looked very much like an oversized pet door, allowing the rotting creatures to stream through the gateway.

'They can't climb can they?' James peered down at the crawling mass below them.

'I have no idea. I haven't actually done this before.' Sarah moved back from the edge, crossing to the opposite side of the roof, trying to figure out their next move.

'Uh, what if they can climb on top of fallen zombies?'

'What?' She stood and walked back, peering over the edge beside him. The force of the group had pressed in to the point where they seemed to overlap; the newest creatures through the door stood on top of the fallen creatures that went before them, each creating a layer that allowed the zombies behind them to find a higher ground. The stained, dripping teeth and clawed fingers reached closer with each wave. Sarah back-pedalled away from the edge.

'Okay, so apparently they can climb, and we have to go,' she babbled, eyes locked on the edge of the roof, watching for the first fingers to reach the rooftop. She pulled into a crouch and shuffled backward, dragging the bags with her.

James had torn his eyes away from the group below, snagging the handle to his own pack and hauling it over to where Sarah knelt at the far side of the roof. A rolling growl shook the air and Sarah whipped her head around.

James raised his hand. 'Sorry! Not a zombie. It's just that we haven't eaten since yesterday.'

Sarah hadn't noticed her own hunger until James mentioned it, and now she suddenly felt it keenly. 'Well, we can't go back and raid the break room now. We'll have to wait till we get home.'

Sarah walked the length of the roof. From the side she could see the horde of zombies that continued to pour through the newly opened door. At the back, the roof overlooked the road that ran behind the shop. Directly below the three metre high roof was concrete, dashing Sarah's hopes of a quick drop into bushes or onto a conveniently waiting car. She scowled. There had been a four-wheel drive in the car park alongside the building, but that left them exposed to any zombie positioned well enough to see the movement. She scrubbed a hand across her eyes. They would have to risk it and hope that the noise and mess of activity in the courtyard kept the attention away from them.

A length of rope lowered the bags to the ground quietly behind the building. James led the way down, returning to the roof above the car and lowering himself down. The faint pop of the dinted roof under his weight sounded remarkably loud in their ears.

Pausing briefly to make sure it had gone unnoticed, Sarah followed, taking care to rest her weight on the same dents before jumping to the ground. Unable to resist glancing into the car, she could smell the odour of groceries spoiling slowly in the hot sun seeping from the partially open window. They regrouped at the wall where they had dropped their loot, crouching below the line of the car. The distinct scrabbling had reached the tin roof now. It was time to go. The street stretched before them wide and empty, offering no hiding place from the hungry predators.

'They may just focus on that.' James gestured to the now open door.

Sarah nodded, unsure of how long it would hold their attention. The radio they had set up at the front door clearly hadn't done the job. Hugging the wall, they edged forward slowly, ignoring every nerve in their bodies urging them to speed up.

The closest zombie turned slightly, nose upturned into the hot air. They froze.

'Is it *smelling* us?' James squeaked.

'It's seen us!' said Sarah. 'Run. Take the bags. It's going to bring the others. Go to the end of the street, I'll meet you there!' She fumbled in James's pants pocket.

James managed to look both affronted and panicked at the same time. 'I'm not leaving you,' he insisted.

Sarah gestured impatiently. 'And I'm not sacrificing myself for you.' She pulled out the lighter she had seen him slip into his pocket in the camping store. 'I'm blowing something up,' she smirked. 'I've always wanted to do this.' She turned to the road. 'I'll be with you in a minute,' she assured him. He looked unconvinced but ran across the street.

Sarah moved back to the four-wheel drive, eyes glancing toward the oncoming zombie. It had managed to complete its turn and now faced her, growling low in its throat between snorting breaths. One leg dragged behind, the ankle clearly broken. Its foot still faced the wall and tilted at an alarming angle. The skin across its torso had been raked viciously, deep lines peeling at the skin where it gaped open. Already Sarah could see that others had noticed the new distraction and had started to turn. She ducked low behind the door of the four-wheel drive. The door on her side of the car was unlocked. She popped it open and foraged through the plastic bags, huffing in relief when her hand found the paper bag of flour she had seen earlier. She pulled it out and opened it outside the car. A glance through the window showed the oncoming zombies to be closer now. Three had turned fully and were making their way toward her; the first was about three metres away, hampered only by the broken leg. Tipping the flour into the car, she coughed as powder invaded her throat, the white cloud completely obscuring her sight. Fumbling for the door, she slammed it shut, no longer needing to hide her presence from the predators closing in. She rolled up the paper bag and jammed it in the window crack. Shaky hands gripped the warm metal lighter, flicking the top open. The scratch of torn nails against the side of the car grated at her nerves, the shadows reaching below the car to snatch at her legs. A spark of flame leapt from between her fingers and ate hungrily at the dry paper, catching quickly. As the flame licked up the wick, she threw herself toward the empty road behind her. In her panic, she felt like she was running on wet sand, pushing herself beyond every limit she had as she flew across the black tar and toward the corner that had swallowed James.

The dark bowels of the car swallowed up the flame momentarily and, for a moment, there was nothing; a deafening absence of noise. Then the world exploded into white and pressure and heat and fire. She was catapulted through the air, her left shoulder slamming into a wall, adding a painful dimension to the noise. She lay in a stunned heap, crumpled at the base of the wall.

Slowly the world righted itself; the glaringly white sky was once again where it belonged. Sarah could hear James yelling her name and there was a sharp tug on her arm, pleading with her to get up. She groaned, the pain in her left arm bringing her spinning nauseatingly back to the present. Her ears rang, the earth still threatening to slip to the side. Logically, she knew she was probably experiencing concussion. James hauled her forward, tripping over nothing. Flashes of green and brown threw themselves at her fuzzy brain. James had somehow managed to sling both bags over one shoulder and was hauling the heavy backpack along in his left hand, while his right gripped her wrist tightly. She could see the impact this was having on him, his shoulder dragging low and his back stooped under the weight. The point where adrenaline stopped being enough of a motivation was visible, as one of the bags fell heavily from its perch onto his elbow, dropping him to his knees. Sarah stopped beside him. James was panting but didn't look at her.

In the silence, Sarah reorientated herself. They had managed to clear a couple of blocks, pulling up outside the facade of the Tender Centre her mother frequented. She could see the complicated intersection ahead and the railway crossing that bisected it, with the green railway watchtower sitting guard over it all. Behind them, a steady column of thick smoke billowed high. Nothing else moved on the street. The ever-present growls and snarls continued to fill the air.

James's eyes snapped to hers, all humour gone from his face.

'Never do that again.' His chest heaved. He didn't say anything else, but his white face spoke volumes. Sarah wanted to make a promise to him, but couldn't form the words. She was willing to do far worse to keep her family safe.

She leant to pick up the first bag before dropping it just as quickly, her shoulder screeching in protest, pulling a gasp from her dry throat.

James looked at the packs heaped at their feet. 'I can't carry them all,' he reluctantly admitted. 'We'll have to leave them.'

Sarah scowled and shook her head. 'We need them all. After what we've done to get them, we've bloody well earned them.'

Her eyes skittered around the deserted street, falling on the small delivery truck parked beside the Tender Centre.

James followed her gaze to the truck and he turned to look at her incredulously. 'I thought we agreed we couldn't hotwire cars?'

Sarah smiled. 'We may not have to. If it's a company truck, they could have keys inside the offices.'

James's lip twitched but he conceded the point. He hauled the bags to the truck, as Sarah's shoulder wouldn't let her help. Her fingers had started to swell and she was sure the shoulder was dislocated, but she couldn't fix it on her own. She didn't trust James to try anything.

While he moved the bags, Sarah walked to the narrow door in the front wall and pressed down on the handle. Unsurprisingly, it was locked, but she could hear a soft gasp from behind the door.

'Quickly … 'hind the counter … down … hear us …' Muted words slithered through the thin door, and then Sarah heard someone say, 'We're armed and we will fire. Go away.' The low bass voice wasn't raised but a slight tremor ran through it.

Sarah kept her voice low, casting glances around her. She could see James's brow crease in curiosity as she spoke haltingly to the closed door. 'There's only two of us—we're unarmed. We just want to get home.' As she spoke, she moved to the side of the door. If the people inside were indeed armed, she wanted to take no chances.

'What do you w—'

The gruff voice was cut off by a sweeter alto. 'Anica?'

Sarah jumped at the sound of her mother's name. 'My name is Sarah, but Anica's my mother.' The door opened a sliver. Sarah couldn't make out any features in the dark but then the door opened and a hand tugged her in by her damaged arm, prompting a shriek of pain.

James was walking to join her but was still far enough away

to hear only his sister's side of the conversation before seeing her being pulled into a dark warehouse.

'Sarah!' he called, grabbing at the closing door and yanking it open. He stumbled into the black recess behind the door and over a detritus-covered floor, just as a heavy thud sent tremors through the counter beside him.

'STOP!' Sarah yelled, her voice echoing through the tin building.

James took in the room as quickly as his dilating pupils allowed. Sarah stood with a slender, dark-haired woman. She seemed to be the same age as their mother, her features drawn up into stressed lines that surrounded soft brown eyes. Hiding behind her was a boy around twelve years of age. The wielder of the pickaxe that had narrowly avoided James's skull was a well-built man, maybe a little older than the woman, his hair greying around the temples. Even though the man had lowered the weapon, he maintained a firm grip on the weathered handle.

Sarah spoke into the tense silence. 'This is James, my brother. James, this is Tracey and Andrew—they own the store.'

James considered the large warehouse, which looked more like a garage filled with discarded or unwanted junk. He could see why his mother loved it. He held out a hand to Andrew who took it in a firm shake.

'Were you open on Boxing Day?' he asked the shaken couple.

'No, we weren't.' Andrew shook his head as he rested the axe on the concrete. 'We had a family BBQ down the road. There wasn't any gate or fence to keep them out. The rest of the family is gone. I managed to get Trace and Mick out but I couldn't find our eldest, Michelle.' Tracey let out a strangled whimper and the boy, Mick, buried his face in her skirt. 'This was the only place I could think of that might be secure.' Andrew's voice had a husky tremor to it as he struggled to remain strong for his wife.

Sarah nodded, her hand rested on the grieving woman's

shoulder. 'Do you know where you're going from here?' She directed the question to Andrew.

He shook his head. 'My sister lives in Warragul …' It was obvious that he hadn't planned for anything beyond this and was grasping at straws, trying to keep calm and level-headed.

Sarah shared a look with her brother. He seemed to scowl a little, giving a minute shake of his head. Sarah chose to read the gesture as James's not understanding what her look had meant, rather than an outright disagreement with her plan.

'We're heading to Mum's now. If we could use the truck that's parked outside, we should all be able to make it relatively safely.' She tried to avoid making any definite promises, not wanting to be held responsible for anything that happened to the group.

Andrew seemed thrilled at any alternative and agreed eagerly, nearly pushing Sarah out of the way to get to the office beside them. He emerged from the office with a small bunch of keys.

'I'll drive,' he stated, walking brusquely toward the door.

They gathered beside the truck, pressed tightly against its sides. Andrew unlocked the doors and settled himself in with practiced ease. James and Tracey hauled the backdoor open and pulled the heavy bags into the gaping interior. Securing the door behind them, Sarah climbed awkwardly into the cab. There had been a brief discussion about the seating until James pointed out that Sarah was needed to give directions to the house, and that she would not able to support her arm comfortably in the back. She cradled it tightly to her chest now, fighting off the waves of nausea that accompanied the jarring agony. Mick squashed himself tightly against his father, refusing to separate from the only protection left to him. Andrew pulled the truck into the road, fishtailing in his haste to get his family to safety.

They drove in silence, bumping over the railway tracks violently and skidding around the messy roundabout before a screech of brakes left Sarah gasping in pain and the bags and unsecured passengers slamming into the front of the cargo hold. Muffled protests were heard through the fibreglass and tin partitions.

Sarah stared wide-eyed at what the others in the back couldn't see. The road in front was crowded with the unrestful dead. They weren't quite choking the road completely, but the numbers were more than large enough to hamper the heavy vehicle.

'Take it slow, not slow enough that they can latch on, but enough that you don't make soup,' Sarah suggested.

Andrew shot her a look, his eyes flicking to the pale boy between them. Sarah winced in understanding but felt the truck lurch into movement below her. The creatures had already noticed them and were moving in their direction. She could feel Mick's slight trembling beside her and pulled his head down onto her lap through her haze of pain. He didn't fight her and was surprisingly pliant as she pulled him off his father.

The first thump startled a whimper from the shaking boy on her lap and her arm tightened involuntarily. They came steadily after that—the popping crunch and lurching of the truck turning Sarah's stomach. It was the only noise that broke the silence of the cab. She reached over to turn the radio on to cover the noise.

'Don't bother, it's been busted for a year,' Andrew muttered, eyes fixed on the windscreen.

Distantly she wondered if it was better to see the dead crowds ahead and the smears of blood that arced across the windshield, smeared by the ineffective wipers, or to ride blind in the cavernous belly of the cargo hold, only able to hear the wet crunches and feel the unsettling bumps as the truck eased forward.

They quickly reached the end of the road. Sarah was able to see, through the side mirror, the carnage they had caused, leaving a red carpet stretched out behind them that any horror premiere would be proud to claim. Andrew pressed the brakes down, slowing as they neared the corner. He looked across to Sarah, wordlessly asking about the next turn.

'Oh, ah … straight,' she stammered.

'You sure?' he asked.

Sarah shot him a look. At one time she had driven this route daily. Of course she was sure. Before she had the chance to voice her thoughts, Andrew nodded. Sarah had been so focused on the wet mess behind them that she failed to notice the thick masses that blocked the road ahead, spilling out from the smaller shops around them. The intersection was impassable; hundreds of lifeless eyes locked on the truck that now idled in the street. Opposite the strip of shops that spread for half a kilometre on the left side of the street was the dry, fenced grass of a school oval.

'Sarah! Where?' Andrew snapped at her. She barely spared him a glance, her eyes skittering across the grisly tableau before them. They wouldn't be able to take the truck much further. Visibility was all but gone and the engine had started straining beneath them. She elbowed her good arm hard into the fibreglass behind them, gasping as the vibrations shook her purpled shoulder.

'James!' she panted, hoping her voice would carry enough to give the passengers warning.

'What's wrong? Why did we stop?' he yelled back. Sarah struggled to make out the muted words that filtered through the tin cabin wall.

'Can't get through and the truck's buggered. Have to go on foot. Wait until I give you the word.' She kept her sentences short and clear, hoping that enough got through to clue James in. She turned to Andrew, pushing Mick's head up off her lap in the process.

'Can you drive the truck up to the school? The fence is high enough to keep them out long enough to make it across. Mum's house is only a couple of blocks behind it.'

Andrew nodded, shifting the dying truck into gear and pushing through the growling crowd. Andrew drove the truck onto the footpath, stopping within inches of the high fence. Sarah knocked her elbow into the cabin's back wall, relieved when she heard the scrabbling noise of movement. With Andrew's door blocked by the fence and her side thronged with the dead, Andrew pushed his son out his open window and over the fence. To his credit, the boy landed quietly, although from the height, it looked as though the fall would have hurt. She pushed at Andrew's back, trying to hurry him forward. He joined his son ungracefully on the hard ground and spun back to help his wife, leaning awkwardly over the high fence.

Sarah had pulled herself painfully out the open window and over the fence beyond it. The infected creatures were now crowding together within two metres of the truck. James and Tracey dragged the duffle bags to the fence, heaving them over and onto the ground. Tracey threw herself over the fence, with James and Andrew close on her heels.

Sarah spared a glance at the pressed in crowd reaching out for them over the fence and froze. At the front of the crowd was a zombie still dressed in the tattered scrubs she had been wearing when she died. Sarah could see the familiar ID tag swinging below the line of her belt, dancing in and out of the chain link openings. She snatched it up quickly, recognising the hospital logo as the one she worked for. Sarah couldn't help but compare the aged, solemn face in the photo to the bloated mess before her; there was nothing of the caring nurse left. White eyes peered out from mottled, rotting skin; her hair was half torn from her scalp and her broken teeth parted in a constant snarl. Below the grasping teeth was a choker style necklace that bit into pale, dead flesh. Sarah blinked and realised that it wasn't a necklace—it was a collar, with a small light blinking at her in the front! Sarah grabbed at the closest arm to her, and Tracey gave a squeal and brushed frantically at her arm.

'What's that?' Sarah pointed at the collar and Tracey gasped, a hand flying up to cover her mouth.

'Andrew,' she choked out, reaching to her husband who had already taken the first steps across the oval.

James turned with him. 'Is that … a collar?' he asked hesitantly.

'Okay, so now we have collared zombies. Can we discuss this further when we're behind closed doors?' Sarah pocketed the ID card and wordlessly turned to join the others as they jogged across the field.

It took a further twenty minutes to reach the heavy gate that framed the house. Their progress was slowed by their careful checks of each street they passed.

Sarah frowned when they reached the gate. The bike chain was gone, replaced with a heavy-duty chain and padlock. A stranger stood on the porch, an oddly shaped bow cradled in his arm. He stood at the group's approach, arrow dangling loosely in his fingers.

'Who are you?' His voice was gruff, roughened by years of smoking.

Sarah scowled and ignored the question. 'Why are you in my mother's house?' she asked, the clipped words spitting from her tongue.

'Sarah and James?' the man asked, his tone notably lighter as he replaced his arrow in a quiver at his side and fumbled in his pocket for a single key.

'Yeah.' James hesitated. 'Sorry, who are you?'

'Sorry, I'm Joe.' His menace softened somewhat and he held out a hand to them after he unlocked the chain. The man appeared to be in his late forties, fit, with a full head of white hair that had been cropped short to reveal ice blue eyes. He smiled broadly, stepping aside to allow them through. There was a squeal from the porch as Anica stepped through, a fussing Charlie in her arms, chubby hands grasping toward her father.

James's face split into a grin as he swept his daughter into his arms. Sarah walked through, her right hand cradling her shoulder, and the small family of three brought up the rear, duffle bags in tow.

'Tracey!' Anica gasped softly, thrilled to see her friend in one piece and skipping down the stairs to usher them into the house. Sarah smiled painfully as Joe held the door for her to pass through, and closed it again while remaining outside.

'I'm on watch for another hour,' he explained.

Sarah nodded, too tired to ask for further explanation, hoping her cluelessness wasn't too obvious. Nell gasped when she saw the misshapen mess of Sarah's arm. She placed a hand on it to steer her into a chair. Sarah screamed in surprise when the gentle grip turned hard and the diminutive girl yanked the arm out, wrenching the ball into its socket. Sarah panted softly, turning shocked pained eyes on her possibly now ex-friend.

Nell smiled. 'I work in ED remember?' She patted Sarah's good arm and went to see if there was anything to use as an icepack.

Sarah leaned back in the chair, not seeing anything beyond the black of her closed eyes. It wasn't too long before James shattered her peace as he entered the room once more, Charlie held tight in his arms.

'Where's Bec?' he asked.

# Chapter Nine

A steady, rhythmic thumping woke the bedraggled group the next morning. Rebecca startled violently, jerking into a crouch, wide eyes searching frantically for the source. Her eyes fell on Seth, who was camped in an office chair, coffee cup permanently fixed to his hand. His asp twitched where it lay in a tight fist across his knees. His eyes remained fixed on the security door they had shut the previous day.

'They've been at it for a while. I think the noise and accumulated smell finally tipped them off.'

Three blurred figures were pressed against the glass, body parts smacking into the door. The glass had been completely obscured in places by a gory red.

'Can they get in?' she asked.

Seth shook his head, turning to face her for the first time that morning. 'Not this many, I think. The door should hold against three. It's the crowd behind them that has me worried.'

Now that it had been mentioned, Rebecca could make out the constant movement beyond. A sea of misshapen figures was steadily approaching the noisy trio.

'We need to get back to the police station and from there head into the city. This place won't be secure for long.' Seth stood smoothly, and the motion was enough to rouse the others.

'Can't we stay at the police station?' Sue's frightened voice drilled into the conversation.

'If we stay in the police station, we'll have the same problem that we do now, maybe worse, given the glass walls along the front. Our best bet is to get in and see what we can find before moving on to find the refugee centre.'

'The Old Gaol.' Karen's voice was controlled and soft.

'Guns do sound good if we're heading out there,' Peter muttered. Sam and Luke nodded their agreement.

Seth looked at Karen. 'We need something to break through under the station. Anything like that you know of around here?'

'You might find something in the old maintenance shed, but it's at the far end of the yard, and we use newer machinery now,' she replied pensively. She walked over to the desks, rummaging through the drawers until she emerged with a set of keys. 'There are two entrances to the yard—the side door here …' She nodded to the sliding door that exited onto the platform. '… and a service door at the back of the offices. The offices are separated from this building by a passenger bypass tunnel that's always open.'

'Is there a map of the station?' Seth asked.

'Not a map, no. There is a satellite shot though. Would that help?'

'That's fine. I just need to be able to see where the shed is in relation to the building.'

Karen returned quickly, the framed photo in her arms. Luke brushed off the desk to make room for it.

'The shed is at the far end here.' She pointed to a small square that leant against the fence on the far side of an extensive stretch of open ground. It looked to be several metres from the building they huddled in; not far on a normal day, but without knowing what waited for them, the distance seemed daunting. Karen seemed to sense the shift in the group's mood and spoke up, to Seth's relief.

'There's a corridor that runs from the door behind us to the passenger bypass. That's about a metre across. The door beyond that will be locked but we have the key. The corridor continues to the service door that accesses the yard.' Her finger traced the path through the building as she spoke. Seth's eyes flicked over to the thumping forms behind the door and up to the security camera above it.

'Do the security cameras cover the service yard?' he asked.

Karen looked stumped. 'Uh … I think so,' she said uncertainly. 'I generally only see it in passing. It's not really my area.' She shrugged apologetically.

'They do.' Luke's quiet, steady voice broke into the conversation. 'Johnny was showing me how to work them before …' He broke off, eyes drifting to the congealing mess on the floor before snapping back to Seth.

'Do they run on mains power or auxiliary? Can you turn them on?' Seth asked.

Luke moved over to the bank of monitors, crouching to pull off a panel near the floor. 'Most new security feeds run off the generator in case of blackouts.' He fiddled with something that Seth couldn't see and the monitors flickered to life with a small whine. Two of the monitors showed the crowded car park and the milling creatures that looked to be focused on the front door of the station; two cameras exposed the platform from either end with five zombies passing in and out of view; one camera sat just in front of the passenger walkway, the brickwork of the arch flirting with the lens. There was another camera over the yard that seemed to be clear but the view was restricted, showing just one side of the aged shed in the back.

'Can these be moved?' Seth asked, frustrated at the blind spots.

'Only manually, and they're fixed behind a dome.' Luke frowned and Seth rested a hand on his shoulder.

'This is good,' he reassured him. 'It's more than we had before.' He looked at the empty yard. 'We need to move fast, the yard looks clear for now, but there's no telling how long that will last for.' He stood quickly, moving to the door and nudging it open gently. The others snatched up their makeshift weapons and followed him, Sue nearly tripping over his heels in her eagerness to remain close. They walked down the dim corridor to the barely visible door that led onto the bypass tunnel.

The door opened silently on well-kept hinges, revealing a clear space beyond. Echoing growls and snarls bounced off the brick arches and a foul odour caused them all to physically recoil. Sue snorted and covered her face with her hand and Rebecca had to do the same.

Plucking the keys from Karen's grasp, Seth strode across the narrow gap, eyes darting from side to side as he kept track of the nearest zombies. He had the door open quickly, and stood aside for the others to barrel past him into the next corridor. One of the creatures, an elderly woman, had seen the mad dash and altered her course to target the shadowed arch. The ravaged silhouette was missing an ear, only the torn cartilage remained to show where it had once hung. The exposed bone of the skull shone in the summer heat, flies congregating around the fetid wound like mourners around an open grave. Her skin looked like an ill-fitting suit, hanging limp and dull from prominent bones and the collar that flashed at them from the emaciated neck looked loose enough to slip over her bony shoulder. Seth slammed the door shut, blinking in the sudden dark.

'Collared?' he muttered absently.

'What?' Karen called back over her shoulder. She had already moved to the next door that would lead them to the yard.

'I think it was collared,' said Seth.

'What the hell are you talking about?' Rebecca asked, stress making her words sharper than she intended and she winced apologetically.

Seth turned from where he still looked blankly at the closed door to face the group. 'That … thing had a collar on its neck.' He cast around for the correct pronoun.

Sam cocked his head to the side. 'Like a dog collar?' he asked.

'Like a tracking collar, for dingoes, or something,' Seth clarified.

'Why would someone be tracking those things?' Rebecca asked.

Seth looked as confused as she sounded. 'I don't know. They might be just randomly recording the spread?' he muttered, wrenching his attention back to the next door.

Peter suddenly perked up. 'What if it's something more nefarious? Like someone experimenting … using this to test something?'

Sue shot him an impatient glare. 'It's not a movie,' she spat out.

'It's not important,' Seth interrupted. 'Let's just not get dead … that's what's important right now.' He turned to Karen. 'They've already started heading this way. I want us to be on the other side of the tunnel when they inevitably block it off.' The key skittered across the top of the lock before slotting in jerkily. Seth opened the door a crack, sharp sunlight spilling in to the dark room.

'It looks clear still. The only other access is from the tracks.' He shot a look at Karen to confirm this and she nodded. He looked back to the dry grass that stretched to the tiny shed. It looked to be little more than a brown tinderbox, its splintered, unpainted panels oozing neglect from every sun-baked rust patch. The only thing that looked cared for was the new padlock that glinted sharply in the evening sun.

'Does one of these open that?' He jerked the keys a little, the sharp jangle sitting harshly in their ears.

'Ah, no. That needs a master set.' Karen sounded worried.

'Shouldn't be a problem.' Seth brushed her concern off gently, eyeing the weathered boards. The yard was still quiet. There was no movement or sudden increase in the ambient growling to set him on edge. He turned his head to the group behind him. 'Stay here and keep the doors open,' he murmured before he bolted out the door, across the open yard, and barrelled into the side of the shed. The momentum pushed him through the aged wood with a crash and into a sprawling heap on the concrete slab. The rolling growl took on a menacing tone as the sound of breaking wood and tools crashing on concrete echoed across the yard and through the large platform's tunnel. A cursory glance showed the few remaining tools littered around him. Seth anxiously looked toward the cavernous railway tunnel where he could see movement nearing the entrance. He snatched up two of the pick axes and a sledgehammer, giving up the rest as a lost cause. He ran back to the open door, waved forward by a frantic Karen. The tools swung awkwardly as he tried to juggle them into a manageable armful while maintaining his speed. A vicious snarl tore through the air beside him before he saw the creature that had been hidden by the open door. Karen shrieked but managed to hold the door open for him, despite Sue's screams of 'Shut the door! Don't let it in!' Seth took a step backward before dropping the pick axes and swinging the sledgehammer in a fluid motion. The mangled head twisted with a sickening snap, leaving it hanging at an impossible angle. Yet the thing kept coming at him and he froze at the surreal sight, the creature unfazed by what should have been a fatal injury.

Rebecca's cry pulled him back to his senses. 'The head! *Seth!*'

He swung hard across its chest, sending it crashing to the ground, from where it attempted to pull its mangled body toward him. Seth brought the mallet down, turning the skull into a pulpy mess as the creature finally lay still.

Sue was crying loudly now. The others were still calling to him and he felt Luke's hand pulling at his sleeve. Peter snagged his other arm while Sam stood outside the door, Karen still holding it open behind him. Sam had picked up the discarded tools and now faced the platform tunnel where a steady stream of milky-eyed figures spilled out of the gloom into the open yard.

Seth forced his thoughts back to a functional state. He herded the boys back beyond the door and slammed it shut behind them. They moved quickly past the offices to the door that opened onto the passenger bypass. Seth inched it open, just enough to reveal the crowded, seething mass beyond. He shut the door again; the adrenaline that had shaken him so badly still coursed through his system. Sam and Peter stood white-faced at his shoulder. Sue and Luke stood behind them, clueless as to what was going on. Karen and Rebecca came to their own conclusions.

'We can't get through there, can we?' Karen asked dully. Seth shot her a sharp look, not liking the despondence that had seeped into her tone.

'Is there roof access?' he asked, frustrated.

'Not for years. The wires, pipes, everything went through roof.' She shook her head.

Seth scanned the room, cataloguing what he had to use. A scattering of simple desks and upturned chairs stood as a memorial to the workers who had once sat there. He hefted the nearest desk with one hand, testing the weight.

'How wide is the passage?' he asked absently.

'About a metre and half,' Karen replied, confusion creasing her brow.

Seth pulled sharply on the single draw under the desk, spilling its contents across the floor and tossing the empty draw into the far corner.

'What are you doing?' Sam asked, shocked at the destruction.

'Making a shell,' Seth said simply, not looking up from his task. He upended the desk so it rested on its side before repeating the action on the next desk. He laid them on their sides with their legs toward each other, before looking up and smiling. 'Did you never play forts as a kid?' He frowned, looking at the legs. 'Have you still got that tape?' he asked.

'I …Yes!' Sam shot forward, fumbling at his pocket, thrusting the roll into Seth's hand.

Seth wound the thick tape around the legs. He left the front open, breaking a chair apart to tape the seat to the desk legs, providing a shabby attempt at protection for the back. He shoved the desks against the wall beside the door and gestured for the group to climb into the cavity.

Sue scowled as she squashed her slender frame into the middle of the group. Seth and Karen stood at the front and Luke and Peter crowded in behind them. Rebecca and Sam pressed into the back. At Seth's barked out orders, everyone hefted the bulky mass of tape and wood to shoulder height. Sue refused, arms tucked under her armpits as she mumbled something about fingernails and dead manicurists.

At shoulder height, the desks provided a fairly secure wall most of the way around. The back was not completely sealed off, allowing Sam to see the room beyond through the ill-fitting cracks and gaps. From their knees down, they had no protection between them and the swarm outside.

Rebecca heard the soft click that indicated Seth had opened the door. The bright slash of sunlight and the fetid air caused her to bury her nose in her shoulder. Seth forged into the seething mass, barrelling through snatching fingers and greedy hands that crept over the tops of the desks and wormed through the cracks. Sue was squealing, her panicky shrieks breaking through the guttural groans and hissing snarls. A thud and a lurching halt was the only warning Rebecca had of their arrival at the next door. She could hear the scratch of metal on metal as Seth searched once more for the lock, muffled curses drifting over the shoulders of those in front.

A heavy dull pain jerked her attention downwards. The torn remains that made up one half of a young woman had sunk its yellowing teeth into the bandage that ensconced her leg. The vice-like pressure was enough to leave her gasping at the pain. The ruined face worried the bandage away from the skin. Rebecca picked up her free foot, driving the heel of her sneaker into the side of the face, knocking it free from her leg. She drove her heel into the thin facial bones, stomping hard, again and again, leaving lumps of brain matter and shattered bone amongst the tangle of matted brown hair on the concrete below. The desk jerked forward violently, pulling her weight onto her now throbbing leg. Her stifled gasp drew a concerned frown from Sam, who stood sandwiched between her and the back of the desks, his attention split between her and the questing fingers seeking them out.

The room was swallowed by the dark as the door was pushed closed, the slavering horde halted from their advance into the small room. They dropped the desks to the floor, the crash echoing loudly in the small room as the group clambered from the ruins. Seth had already moved into the front office area, depositing his new tools on the floor by the door that he and Rebecca had come through initially.

'Is everyone okay?' he asked, as the group trailed in behind him. Each nodded and Rebecca checked her calf, wincing as the tape pulled away from the tender skin. She rubbed a hand gingerly over the area, checking for blood or breaks but finding only the already healing scratches from the broken window in the tyre shop. Seth levelled a serious look at her.

'I'm fine,' she insisted. 'It's just bruised. The skin wasn't broken.' She stood, wincing as her weight settled on the limb. She took a hesitant step, testing the leg.

'Let's just go.' Her voice was soft but determined as she opened the door and started down the stairs.

Sue had been relatively quiet, keeping her opinions to glares and the odd contemptuous facial expression; now though, she had apparently reached what miniscule limits of patience she had, no longer able to continue without voicing her opinion. 'Why can't we just stay here?' She crossed her arms and moved to the far corner, refusing to look anyone in the face. 'The building is closed off and I'm tired … and scared …' she added in a small voice. 'We have food and water right here, and I really, *really* don't want to go out there!'

Seth pointedly ignored her, taking up the cumbersome tools and following Rebecca down the stairs. Karen looked torn between following them and comforting the sullen blonde. She waved the boys down the stairs and turned to her.

'How long do you think this food and water will last?' she asked firmly. 'No one is coming. There will be no more food delivery, and the walls will not hold up forever. You can stay if you like, but if you plan on living, I suggest you follow those who have a better idea of how to survive.' Karen stood and joined the group at the bottom of the stairs, sighing in relief as Sue's footsteps followed her down into the shadowed cellar.

The tunnel seemed colder as they walked through it once more. Seth found the area he had been working on quickly and passed the pick to Sam.

'We'll start off and pass to Luke and Rebecca in ten minutes, then Karen and Pete.' He didn't bother mentioning Sue, already anticipating the reaction he was likely to get.

Sam grinned, swinging the axe between his legs and pulling it up over his head, burying the sharp tool in the crumbling tunnel roof, sending clumps of cement and fountains of dust raining down on the group below. They scrambled backward, coughing and cursing.

'Sorry!' he spluttered, his face and hair grey. Seth shook the dust from his eyes and stepped up, swinging his own axe into the same spot, a small cavity forming under the attack. Sam swung once more, with this strike pulling a large chunk to the floor. The resounding boom as the chunk hit the wooden floor was drowned out by a deep guttural boom as the air around them exploded into a wave of debris, burying them in a tomb of concrete and steel. Nothing moved except for the column of dust dancing in the exploratory beams of light tumbling down through the ruined floor above.

# Chapter Ten

The house was a flurry of activity as the inhabitants worked to organise the goods they had gathered and unceremoniously dumped on the living room floor. Sarah and James were still acclimatising to the changes in the small group; though it was clear James's thoughts remained focused on his absent wife.

Joe was one of four newcomers they had been introduced to in the days following their return. He had apparently lived at the end of the street for years, a retired truck driver, who had settled into a semi-reclusive lifestyle, only communicating with the outside world via his radio. Joe fancied himself a mechanically-minded man and had spent his time playing with the radios that James and Sarah had brought back, fixing one in the house and the other in the ute, one of two vehicles Joe had managed to source from neighbouring yards. Every now and then he would scan through the channels, listening for any more information or a hint of life beyond the high gate they were trapped behind. The ute and the small campervan, the other salvaged vehicle, had been reinforced with sheets of corrugated iron, encasing the glass on either side, and connected via a rough hinge at the top to allow access the doors. Chicken wire layered the front and back windows securely, doubled over and bolted to the frame where possible.

Joe and James had driven through the neighbourhood in the ute, looking for other survivors. They had found only two houses with signs of life, both secured like their own behind tall iron gates. Unsurprisingly, none of the inhabitants had opted to talk to the unknown men at the gates.

Some of the houses they'd walked past had suffered broken windows. Whatever remained of the inhabitants was now likely smeared in macabre patterns throughout the house. The buildings that were untouched suggested that their occupants had been amongst the opportunistic shoppers caught up in the horror of the Boxing Day sales. They had scoured what houses they could, emptying them of the food and equipment they thought might be useful. These things now took up the majority of floor space within the house.

The role of sorting the goods into their proper places had fallen to Sarah, Anica and the two international students, Lucy and Amy. The girls had turned up on the doorstep after the house they were in was taken over by the ravenous creatures. They were quiet, occasionally speaking in broken English, but they followed directions well and Nell had taken to staying with them, avoiding the heavy atmosphere that hung over the rest of the home.

The last addition to their group was Justin, a fairly short, middle-aged man. What little Sarah had seen of him seemed familiar, but she couldn't place him. So far, he had done little more than sit on the couch with his head in his hands. The only reason they knew his name was the thick security nametag on the lapel of his coat, the one item of clothing that covered his pyjamas. James and Joe had brought him back after one of their first forays into the streets. He had been walking aimlessly along the freeway that led toward Ballarat and they had nearly taken his head, thinking him to be infected. Then he'd looked at them—not with the dead blind eyes of the zombies, but with the look of one lost in his own misery. They had pulled him into the car and brought him home, and he hadn't moved from the couch since.

It was Sarah who had decided to see what could be salvaged

from the aged care home where she had worked for years. Her purple, swollen shoulder was a constant source of pain and she knew she needed to get something to take the edge off.

Agitated fingers toyed with the hard plastic—a small card that would open the drug room door. She tapped it thoughtfully and stood, deciding that action was preferable to the anxious waiting they all seemed to be fidgeting through.

James had been overly protective of Charlie since he had learned of his wife's absence, keeping her in sight even while working on the car alongside Joe. Not wanting to risk taking a distracted James to clear out the nursing home, Sarah dragged a reluctant Nell to the ute, throwing a quick explanation over her shoulder as she passed Joe.

The streets were void of life or any semblance of it as they moved through the back roads, the air heavy with the thick, ever-present stench that they barely noticed anymore. Every now and then they passed a forlorn figure that followed their progress with dead eyes, walking, in some cases quite quickly, but inevitably falling behind the car. Several dogs ran free in the street, some bold enough to tear at the meaty legs on offer, uncaring of the flies that accompanied each mouthful.

Sarah and Nell pulled up out the front of the aged care home, carefully checking the car park for threats before climbing out. They could see a female pressed up against the window of a locked car, her movements sluggish as she beat uncoordinated hands against the glass.

The home's automatic door slid open at their approach, and they walked the familiar halls, each step slow and cautious. The bloody carpets and gore-smeared walls bore witness to the horrors that had touched the place of respite.

Sarah shuddered, thinking of the helpless bed-ridden and chair-bound residents she had cared for, wincing as the metallic tang of blood clawed at her throat. 'Let's make this quick. I don't want to spend any longer here than we need to.'

Nell nodded wordlessly, pointedly not looking at the discoloured walls. The dining room was a massacre; chairs and tables were overturned, and remnants of clothes, some of them recognisable as nursing scrubs, littered the floor between pools of blood and torn flesh.

Sarah closed her eyes, taking shallow breaths as she walked quickly to the nurse's station, fumbling with the acquired swipe card and swinging open the drug room door. She found the keys to the drug cupboard on the trolley inside the door, sighing in relief at the neat containers of painkillers on the shelf. She opened the one on top, swallowing two dry before hurriedly piling every box she could find into an empty garbage bin that sat under the nurse's desk. Antibiotics, painkillers, even eye drops—everything was scooped up into the black-lined bin.

A persistent noise caught Sarah's attention—a steady beeping coming from the bank of computers that ringed the desk. She turned to see Nell stooped before one, her frame almost obscuring the screen's flashing light.

'Why would Esther's room be buzzing?' Nell asked, not turning from the screen.

'Faulty wiring maybe?' Sarah shot back, not willing to spend any more time in the slaughterhouse. 'Can you help me move these to the car so we can start on the store room?' She awkwardly shuffled the bags to the tray of the ute now, eager to distance herself from the scene around her. On her second trip back she realised Nell wasn't making any moves to help her.

'Sarah!' she heard Nell call down the passage. 'Guess what I found!'

She glared at the mousy girl as she rounded the corner. Nell wasn't alone. Esther, the youngest resident of the home, was following unsteadily in her wake.

Esther had been admitted into the home for schizophrenia, her quiet cheer and usually childlike personality setting her apart from the dementia that was predominant in the other residents. She was a quiescent 48-year-old, who made thrice-daily trips to the kitchenette for a cup of tea as an excuse to catch up on the gossip with every person she passed. Now, though, her face was pulled into a frown and she didn't lift her eyes from the floor as she approached. Sarah was astounded. How had she survived all this? Her eyes swept over the woman, scanning for any sign of injury. High on Esther's right arm, just below her shoulder, a brown stain trailed its dripping fingers down the dirty blouse, although Esther seemed not to notice it. She stepped back, prepared to tell Nell to leave Esther here when something made her pause. The drying patch. If it were an older bite, surely there would have been some sign of infection by now? Could there have been some other reason behind the wound? Sarah stepped toward them.

'Esther? What happened to your arm?' She kept her voice steady and calm.

'Jan bit me. I hit her and ran and hid in my room.' She looked up now, peering at Sarah suspiciously. 'Are you going to bite me too?'

'No love, I'm not.' Jan had been a long-term nurse that she had known well and who would never have left her residents by choice. And this meant an infected person had bitten Esther. Could something have altered the spread of the virus? She voiced her thoughts to Nell.

'This virus attacks the brain, right?' Nell mused. 'Maybe the neural pathways in a patient with mental health issues are different? Maybe there's a block, or something that is stopping the virus from taking hold completely.'

'Like a natural defence?' Sarah suggested. Nell nodded slowly, although she looked unconvinced.

They decided fairly quickly that despite the risk of taking on an extra person with the possibility of instability, they couldn't leave her behind. The storeroom was mostly empty now; the extra dressings Sarah had taken were crammed into every spare corner the ute had to offer, even taking over the passenger foot well. They decided they would need to take another car from the scant offerings in the car park, settling on a four-wheel drive parked in the wheelchair space. Its front door hung open and a purse emptied onto the ground beside it, with the keys thankfully on top. Nell stayed in the ute with Esther while Sarah climbed into the new car.

The grounds were silent as they drove past the front gate, only once stopping at the sight of movement. A shambling, slippered figure had passed through the bushes, its ataxic gait causing them both to stop. Sarah pulled the off-roader alongside the ute as they assessed the situation.

'Are you sure?' Nell had asked, leaning out the window to whisper, 'If it's not, we can't leave it.'

'Uh … yes?'

'You don't sound sure.'

'Well, I can't help it if the bloody things look and sound like a dementia patient … oh, never mind, it's missing half its face. Let's go.'

They didn't look too closely at the few figures they passed after that.

The trip home was blissfully silent as Sarah was left alone with her thoughts. The car's windows were rolled up tightly to quieten the distant growls. The few stragglers that tried to follow them were unable to keep up with the vehicles' speed and were quickly left behind as they covered the distance to the house.

They pulled up between the tall gates that Joe opened at their approach. James was holding his crowbar in one hand, the other cradling Charlie while he kept watch on the porch. Esther pulled herself out of the cab of the ute, but hung back, uncertain of her welcome. Sarah and Nell unloaded the ute, enlisting the help of Alex and Joe so they could start sorting the haul.

The mountains of food, drink and dressings tumbled across the floor as the last bag was pushed into the room. They separated the supplies into the cars outside, choosing carefully so as not to take up precious space.

As James stood on the porch fingering the heavy bar, he grew more and more pensive. Once again the lack of distraction was pulling his thoughts back to his absent wife. In the absence of distractions, the tense silences grew longer in the house. James's glances to the front gate became more frequent as he held onto his quiet daughter.

A distant explosion took everyone by surprise. The windows in the small kitchen shook under the pressure. James dropped the bar as he held his daughter tight and ran to the detached shed behind the house with Sarah and his parents close behind him.

The window on the second floor overlooked the suburban sprawl that stretched between their house and the city. Where the blue of the bay and the imposing granary silos could be seen on a clear day, a thick column of oily black smoke now billowed across the city.

James groped for the windowsill with a shaky hand. Charlie started to cry as she clung to his shirt under his other arm. James's dull eyes stared out at the sky as it bled into clouds of red and black.

Everyone except Justin crowded around the narrow windows, trying to see where the explosion had come from. Loud pops and the occasional burst of flame spoke of an ongoing danger while hiding everything under its choking cloak.

'Bec,' James whimpered, fingers white where they clenched the window frame.

Sarah moved to stand between him and the door, hoping to stop him from having any rash ideas about running to the rescue, but he seemed unable to move.

Amy walked to his side, resting a hand on his shoulder. 'You want I take Charlie?' she offered in her broken English.

James shook his head and closed his eyes, slipping down to slump against the wall, a teary Charlie held in his lap.

'She's not dead,' he murmured into his daughter's sparse hair. 'I'd know if she was … she's not dead.' He lifted red dry eyes to his father. 'Can you just …'

Alex nodded and guided the others from the room, leaving James to comfort himself with his daughter.

# Chapter Eleven

Pain was the first thing that Seth was aware of as fingers of agony danced up his leg. He groaned and a shushing noise tickled his ear as a cool hand rested against his forehead.

'You've fractured your leg and sustained a rather vicious knock to your head. I have some painkillers here for you. They're not as strong as we'd like but it's better than nothing.' A cup was pressed to his lip and cool water trickled down his throat, followed by a small pill and another sip of the much-needed water.

'Where …' He broke off in a fit of coughs before gasping again as his leg seized up at the sudden motion. The shushing came again.

'You're safe. You're in the refugee centre on the pier.'

Seth nodded, cracking an eyelid open, only to close it again when the light threatened to blind him.

'I'd dim the lights but we're not really blessed with a lot of options for that here.' The light voice seemed to laugh at him. 'You're lucky we found you. Our boys were in the university, clearing out the food in the cafeteria, when the petrol station exploded. Fortunately they were in the lower levels. Half the building was wiped out on the city side.'

Seth frowned, forehead creasing in confusion. What explosion? Since when did they have a refugee centre on the pier? He was sure the radio had said Geelong's refugee centre was in the Old Gaol. The woman pressed on with her story.

'The party that found you weren't expecting to find anyone in the wreckage. They … um … they wanted to see what they could get from the police station. It's been locked up until now, and we couldn't get in before, but the explosion gave us a way in. You were all pretty banged up. One of the girls, the young blonde, didn't make it. We're still waiting to see about one of the others. The older woman is the only one awake but she can't talk, for now at least. She got a pretty nasty thump against her throat and we have no way of knowing how bad it's going to be until she's well enough to try talking.' She trailed off, giving him another sip of water. 'I'll let you rest now.'

Seth tried to talk, to ask which girl had died, but he broke into another fit of coughing, again leaving him in agony. The woman rested a hand on his forehead and then walked out of the room. Seth slipped into a restless sleep.

When he woke again, the light in the room was lower, allowing him to open his eyes. The room he was in looked like an office; the windows had no curtains but the sun was low enough not to bother his eyes. He was lying on top of a desk; a layer of towels was all that cushioned his back against the hard desk that he rested on. His right leg was encased in a thick bandage from mid-thigh to ankle and was propped up on a couch cushion. Beneath the bandage, he could see the rough edges of a snapped off chair leg that had been used as a splint. He wriggled his toes weakly, thankful to see that he still could, even when his leg complained at the movement. The room housed one other person who was covered by what Seth assumed were the curtains from the windows. He swung his leg gingerly over the edge and sat on the side of the desk. His head spun as he lifted himself up to see if he recognised the other person. The hair that peeked out the top of the curtain was dirty blonde. He leaned heavily on the chair that sat beside the desk and hopped a little closer, wincing at the pain that fought through whatever drugs were being used to keep it manageable. The face was covered and he leant down slowly to pull the sheet aside. Behind him he could hear footsteps nearing the door. He growled in frustration as his leg screamed at him, stepping back and falling wearily into the chair behind him as the door opened.

'What are you doing up?' The voice sounded oddly angry, although he recognised it as the voice from before.

'I needed some water.' His voice sounded foreign as he spoke, the smoky rasp sounding strange in his ear. 'Where's Rebecca? And Karen, Sue and the boys?'

'The boys are okay,' she said gruffly. 'They all pulled through and they're safe a few doors down.'

Seth made to stand up again, wanting to see them, but the woman's hand pressed down firmly on his shoulder, pushing him back in the chair.

'They, at least, can walk. I'll bring them to you, if you think you can sit still.' She placed a glass of water on the desk beside him and walked from the room, returning shortly with the smiling dirty faces of the three boys.

'I guess I don't know my own strength,' said Sam with a grin.

Seth looked over at the young men in front of him, thankfully not seeing anything too disastrous.

Luke noticed his perusal. 'The worst we got were headaches, and a concussion on Sam's part. Frankly, I have no idea how he made it out at all. He was right underneath when the floor came down.'

'He was cushioned by his ego,' Peter interrupted.

Luke slapped him. 'We saw Karen; she's doing pretty good considering.' He fell silent, shooting a look at his twin. 'Bec ...' he paused. 'She was hit pretty bad. But she's still alive!' He hurried on as he saw Seth start to draw the wrong conclusion. 'But she hasn't woken up yet. Sue didn't stand a chance.' He frowned. 'They said that part of the floor fell right where she was sitting.'

Seth was silent. The thought that one of the group had died weighed heavily on his conscience. He could see that the boys hadn't had time to fully come to terms with the new loss that seemed to compound the loss of their own families. But in the unfamiliar surroundings and the unknown particulars of this new group they had found themselves hauled into, he knew they wouldn't feel comfortable enough to address it.

'Where are we?' he asked, to take their minds off Sue's death.

'On the pier,' Sam said quietly. 'They've closed the gates and run a fence from the beach down either side of the car park. No other survivors can get near the gates because of the hundreds of zombies that don't ever seem to leave the front, but at least there's only one entrance to watch. The only access seems to be by boat, going directly from further down the shore to the restaurants here at the back.'

Luke took over the narration. 'They gave us a quick walk-through. They have plenty of access to fresh fish, and there are water tanks on the roof. The dining area of the restaurant is full of refugees. They didn't take us through the kitchens though. Apparently it's too crowded to show everybody.'

Peter was quiet. Seth looked at him but he shuffled his eyes away guiltily.

'Pete?' he asked.

'I heard … growling in one of the back rooms near the kitchen …' He broke off, shooting a hesitant look at his twin.

'What was that look for?' Seth asked.

Peter grudgingly cleared his throat. 'Just, some of the refugees said we needed to leave. That some people who were here in the beginning had gone missing.'

'Maybe they don't want to be crowded any further? And the lady did say that some people had turned and had to be put out-side.' Sam scowled.

Peter just glared back. 'Don't make excuses for them. You know the whole place feels wrong. And what about the "off limits" offices? And the growling?'

Seth didn't like the implication; he clicked his fingers, making sure he had Peter's full attention. 'It sounds like you think the people running this place have something big to hide.'

Peter shifted his weight. 'I don't know what I'm saying. I heard what I heard, I saw what I saw, and I know that some of the people keep talking about people that go missing, from *inside* the pier.'

Seth wasn't given to trusting easily at the best of times, so he was more than happy to assume the worst and prove his suspicions wrong later.

'From here on out, let's be paranoid. This might be coincidental, or it might be something serious, we don't know. For now, pay attention to everything and watch what you say around people you don't know.' He made sure to look each of the boys in the eye. 'Keep your eyes open.' He leaned back again, wincing at the change in position. 'Where are the girls?' he asked.

'Next door. They kept these two offices as the first-aid rooms.' Sam waved a hand toward the right hand wall.

'Can you get your hands on something I can use as a crutch?' he asked.

'There is a set of crutches … a couple actually. They have a heap of ownerless equipment in Karen's room.' The way Peter sneered at the word 'ownerless' implied the owner did not need them any longer, and not because they had been miraculously healed.

'Can you find a set to fit me?' he asked. 'And check on the ladies?'

As they left the room, Seth allowed the pained grimace he had been holding back to slip across his features.

'Did the pain meds wear off already?' The voice startled him and he shot a look at the blonde head under the sheets that had been chased from his mind by the boys' visit. A round female face peered back. Her long hair was the same shade as Rebecca's with eyes of a darker muddy brown.

'How much of that did you hear?' he demanded, quickly on the offensive.

'Enough to know that I can help.' She stood on short bowed legs, her snubbed nose level with where his belt would have been if he could stand easily. She held a hand out. 'I'm Helena.'

'Seth. What do you mean help?' he asked, shaking her hand.

'Your boy is right, they're running tests here. There's no one to regulate them anymore, see?' Her face darkened. 'Two days into hell and morals have gone to shit. I think they may be testing to see how it is transmitted and how far it spreads from a set point. Not on everyone, you understand. They want to see what happens if you're on certain medications, or have another health issue.' Her face twisted into a cynical scowl. 'Can't go around raising suspicions among the refugees. If you watch though, you'll notice that you won't find any old people here, or anyone less than "normal".' She crooked her fingers for emphasis. 'If a subject takes, they're tagged and released back outside the gate …' She trailed off. 'It's why I'm in here. I accidentally saw the front office during preparation on my first day. They've turned it into a lab. Current acute-type patients seem to be exempt from testing, probably because they want to control all the pathogens that a person contracts. So I came down with a conveniently nasty cold, though I'm sure they'll catch on eventually.'

Seth was shocked and he schooled his features carefully. 'Why though? What's the motive? Isn't it bad enough to have dead people running around eating living people?'

Helena lowered her voice as she stumbled haltingly through half formulated ideas. 'I think, from what I've seen, the people here are part of the reason this thing exists in the first place. Their work is far too advanced to be starting all of this now. I believe the ones in charge here may be scientists. It's certainly no refugee centre. The most qualified person I've met on the main floor is a waitress.' She shot a dark look to the door. 'They're good at covering their tracks, and eliminating or avoiding any potential threats. Considering how close we are to the police station, I would have thought to see at least one cop here if this was a genuine refugee centre.'

'How do you know so much?' Seth didn't think she had a hand in the alleged experiments, but the way she spoke seemed to hint at a higher education.

'I work in the pathology lab,' she said, not taking offence at the question.

They stopped speaking as the door opened, Sam swinging through on a pair of crutches, Peter and Luke trailing in after him.

'Rebecca's awake. She and Karen don't want to hang around here for long,' Luke said, as he leaned against the desk slowly so as not to jar Seth's leg.

Seth took the crutches and stood, trying out his balance on them. He winced. Luke shot a curious glance at the short blonde and back to Seth, who still managed to look imposing even when standing with crutches.

'She knows … more than we do at least.'

'Will she be coming with us then?'

Seth wasn't surprised that they had all come to the conclusion to leave without discussing it as a group first.

'I will,' Helena informed them. 'There's no way I'm staying here to play rhesus monkey to their mad scientist.'

'Luke, show me to the ladies please,' Seth said, as he hobbled out the door, stepping aside to let the fair boy pass. Luke opened the door next to his, letting the group file in before shutting it again.

Rebecca sat against the far wall with Karen beside her, nursing a heavily bandaged neck and a black eye. Rebecca's head and right arm were now wrapped up and the bandages on her legs had been replaced with fresh wraps. Seth winced at the damage and lowered himself into a nearby chair, groaning as he did so. Rebecca was first to speak up.

'How are we getting out?' she demanded, her eyes still a little unfocused. Ideally Seth would have preferred to stay in one spot for the time being, to allow for healing, but this was unfriendly territory, and as much as he felt for those left behind, his priority was to this group first. Helena was the one who took the floor.

'I've been looking for a way off the pier ever since I saw the kitchen.' She tried to repress a shudder. 'The gate is constantly swamped with zombies and they keep a patrol on the pier itself. The only way off is by boat, or swimming, and I don't fancy your chances in the water.' She eyed Seth's leg critically.

'Do you know anything about boats?' he asked.

'I know they go in the water.'

Seth narrowed his eyes.

'Do I *look* like I know my way around a boat?' she shot back.

They were stopped from further conversation when they heard the door to the other office swing open.

'She's not here!' They strained to hear the hushed angry voices and Helena's face drained of colour. 'He's gone too!'

'What do you think she told him?' asked the female voice. There was silence as the door swung shut and then steps covered the short distance between the rooms.

Seth gestured to Helena to hide and she scrambled under the desk. He didn't stand up. Instead he handed his crutches to Luke and Peter and gestured for them to stand behind the door. They were barely in place before the door swung open. The petite brunette nurse he had barely seen entered the room, followed by a bespectacled man in a suit. As their angry eyes swept the room Seth smiled disarmingly.

'Is something wrong?'

The woman scowled. 'I told you to stay put,' she snarled, the welcoming veneer thrown aside.

'I was unaware I was a prisoner,' said Seth, which seemed to unsettle her a little.

'You're not a prisoner; you're a patient who needs to be resting.' She struggled to regain the upper hand, her unease in the situation apparent.

'I'm a patient who wants to see how his friends are going.'

A sneeze from under the desk caused a collective jump. The man, who until now had been silent, stepped forward.

'Hand her over. She's been infected and we have to put her out.'

'I saw no signs of infection. I'm sure she's fine.' Seth tensed, his eyes flicking to the two hidden behind the door.

'I ran the test myself, sir. She needs to be quarantined from the group.' The man was growing agitated, inching further inside the door, the woman close behind him. Helena had scooted out from behind the desk and stood close to Seth.

'I'm not!' Helena's voice had picked up a barely discernible quaver. She turned to Seth, willing him to believe her. Karen moved beside her to offer silent support.

The man's face turned ugly and his hand whipped to the belt at his side, the woman doing the same. Seth was just able to glimpse the shine of metal before Luke and Peter shoved the door into the pair, pushing them both off balance. The brunette scrambled for the door handle, her fingers slipping as she tried to pull it shut. The gun dropped to the floor and Luke brought his crutch down on the suited man's head, stunning him momentarily. He managed to lift the gun and fire a shot before another heavy blow dropped him to the floor. Peter brought the other crutch down over the head of the woman, who immediately crumpled, unconscious. Luke drove his heel into the man's temple and he slumped beside the woman.

'They will have heard all that! I hope you know where the boats are!' said Seth, as he gestured to the boys to grab the guns.

They passed one to him and started to hand the other to Karen but she held her hands up and shook her head.

'I've never fired one.'

Luke smiled and went to put the gun in his own belt but Helena stopped him.

'Give me that before you shoot your own arse off.' She took it from him and held it tightly in her hand.

Seth looked toward Helena, who had regained her colour somewhat and now stood beside an unsteady Rebecca, helping her keep her balance as she climbed to her feet. Helena didn't speak as she took the lead, walking out the door and leaving Rebecca to lean on Karen. The group followed Helena as she led them away from the offices to a staircase at the far end of the hall. It descended into a well-lit kitchen, the bustle and mess of voices ringing up to them. Karen grasped Helena's arm, aghast at the prospect of entering the kitchen.

'They keep the boats just outside … Easy access to the shore,' Helena whispered.

Thudding footsteps sounded up the steps on the far end of the corridor and Seth pushed forward, forcing the others down the narrow staircase. Helena paused at the foot of the stairs, glancing quickly around the corner. She waved Karen and Rebecca across and they ducked low, running behind a narrow bench that provided a little cover from the kitchen workers. Helena joined them, and peeked over the edge of the desk before jerking her head, signalling for the others to join them. Sam and Peter stood beside Seth as he hobbled across to them with Luke close behind, eyes darting everywhere. A shout came from the offices above them.

'Quickly!' Helena ran to the back door that opened onto a rear jetty. Behind them someone dropped a glass in surprise as each went through the doors as quickly as they could. They heard someone call out angrily from behind, spurring them to move faster.

Seth was in the back. He could hear footsteps pounding down behind them and pulled the flimsy door shut, hanging his weight off the door handle to hinder their access. It wouldn't stop a bullet but it might slow them down a little. Whatever was going on here, it was clear they weren't supposed to catch wind of it.

Helena cried out in relief when she caught sight of the moored boat. The vessel was small, but sufficient for their group. Luke grasped the rope, tugging the small boat into the jetty. The unseen pursuers were pounding against the door as the boat's nose bumped the wooden supports. Shots rang from inside and the lock blew out. Seth released the handle in shock. Sam jumped in to hold the handle for him, as a hand yanked at it from inside. Karen wasted no time jumping down, helping Helena and Rebecca in. Luke and Peter held the boat steady, and supported Seth as he made his painful progress onboard.

Sam struggled to hold the door in his place. Once Seth was seated, Sam released the bucking door and dived into the dangerously rocking boat, kicking hard at the poles to push it away from the pier. The door slammed open into the wall and three men, two in suits and one in a well-used lab coat, spilled onto the slats. The sun glinted off the guns as they were pulled into sight.

Helena pushed the twins toward the wheel. 'GO!' she roared.

Loud pops peppered the air around them, a few bullets boring into the wood of the boat. Instinctively they all ducked. Seth brought the pistol up and fired three quick shots, sending the men on the narrow deck scrambling for cover. Karen hauled the rudder hard to swing the small boat behind the building and toward the open bay. She heard a high-pitched yelp behind them, just as they swept out of sight. The boys pulled hard at the oars, straining to put distance between them and the pier.

'Helena, is there another door on the other side of the restaurant?' Karen's face was creased in thought.

'Not that I saw. I think they'll have to go out onto the front pier to get another shot.'

The boat fell silent save for the purring motor, each passenger craning their necks to look for shadows moving through the building or among the cars on the dock. The shore passed beside them, guiding them past the silent carousel that sat cheerfully against the dour background. They shuddered as the rolling growls and snarls washed over them once more. The silhouettes of the infected seemed to dance slowly around the bollards, creeping through the sharp tooth-like sculptures that clustered between the carousel and the pier. Infected covered the road that sloped down from the city, spilling over the top like herded sheep.

They passed the park and the string of eateries that hid the marina from the pier, the distance and visual block finally allowing them to relax a little.

'Pull in here.' Helena's voice was pained and soft.

Karen spun the rudder to guide the unfamiliar vessel toward the walkway, bumping into poles as she passed them, grimacing at the small yelps of pain behind her. Sam grasped a rope that hung off the end, pulling the boat close to the marina's walkway, and tied it off. He knelt on the hard wooden bench. Seth raised himself just high enough to peer over the edge.

'It's a bit crowded up there. How do you plan on getting past them?' he asked.

'Not past, under,' Helena said through gritted teeth. They all turned to her. She was holding tightly to her side where fresh blood seeped through her torn shirt.

'What happened?' Karen demanded, tugging at Helena's hand to see the damage underneath.

'It's not that bad,' she insisted, resisting the pull. 'Just got a little grazed is all.' She winced as she pressed her hand back to the flesh wound again. 'We need to go under them,' she urged again, pointing to the yacht club on their right. The others looked at her blankly. 'Just trust me,' she growled.

Seth was in no mood to argue, still fighting off the pain that shot up his leg whenever he tried to move.

With another glance at the thronging horde, Rebecca made the decisive call. 'All right, you lead. We're right behind you.'

Helena lowered herself gingerly into the water, thankful that the tide was low enough to allow her to see the bottom. Even in the shallows, the water reached her neck. Blood ribboned from her wound into the bay, prompting Sam to offer his back to keep her out of the water, and she gratefully accepted the help. Seth hung between Peter and Luke. His face was pale, but his eyes remained alert and his hand gripped the gun over Luke's shoulder, the handle digging sharply into the young man's collarbone.

Helena led the small group under the docks to the fenced off yard of the yacht club, forcing them to crouch low in the water under the dock. The yard offered a short respite from the clinging seaweed and the high iron fence kept the other ocean of torn faces safely separated from them. Helena hurried them on, under the Ferris wheel perched above the beach, and into the water once again. The water at their calves churned as the overflow from a large storm drain eddied around them, the large concrete tube disappearing into a black shadow.

The constant trickle of water and the occasional echoed thump from something further up in the tunnels drowned out the growls that had stalked them above ground. The smell of damp and mildew made for a pleasant alternative to the cloying stench of blood and human waste that had often stopped their breath. Helena led them further in with the confidence of a frequent visitor. She ignored the smaller side tunnels that spilled their own water collections into the underground stream. They kept walking straight ahead, the glint of sunlight growing tiny behind them until they walked in near darkness only broken by the tiny strips of light from the street gutters. Every now and then Helena would pause to check the markings on the walls beside the tributary tunnels with the aid of a Seth's tiny torch.

Finally she found a mark that made her smile and, burying a toe into the rough wall, she tried to haul herself up to the higher tunnel, only to gasp and grab her side as she slid into the main tunnel once again.

'Would you mind?' She looked to Sam, gesturing at the tunnel. Obligingly he knelt and offered his knee as a step, and Helena climbed into the elevated tunnel. This one was about half the diameter of the one they had come from and offered a series of iron rungs set into the wall, leading upwards. Helena climbed up the short ladder slowly; her wound had stopped bleeding but her shirt clung to the tacky skin. The top of the ladder was capped with a metal grate. She could just make out the shadows beyond and waited a little to make sure they didn't move. Tentatively, she cleared her throat and rattled the grate sharply, hoping to draw out any threats while they still had a grate between them.

'Hello?' The unexpected voice made her jump and a face suddenly eclipsed the faint light. Helena scrambled to grab the bars before shock sent her falling to the tunnel below. A click preceded the sudden flood of light that illuminated the dank tunnel. Helena's hand flew up to shield her eyes.

'Sorry! Sorry!' The unseen person moved a little to block the light. 'I was a little shocked. I haven't seen another person in three days now … I think. How did you get here? What's it like out there? Is it safe to come out now?' The questions flew thick and fast, not giving Helena a chance to respond.

'Hold on, just … Hang on. Can you help me get this grate up so we can get out of the water? We'll fill you in on everything when we're not underground and soaked.'

'We? Is there more of you?' The voice managed to sound both excited and apprehensive at the thought.

'There are six others—and we have injuries.' Helena could see the figure disappear from view followed by the rough clatter of draws being shuffled through. He came back shortly and slotted something into the grates, leaning on it heavily and prying it up. Dirt, rocks and debris rained around them and Helena dropped her head to shield her eyes.

She stayed like that until the shower stopped. A quick look revealed that the grate had been removed and a hand was now held out to help her up. She took it gratefully, leaning back into the tunnel to call out to the others.

'Are …' She was cut off by a hissed 'Shhh' and then Rebecca stuck her head up through the grate.

'There's something coming down the main tunnel from further in.' Rebecca hesitated, throwing a glance back over her shoulder. 'Seth's not doing well. He passed out while we were getting him over the edge and he's been drifting in and out ever since.' There was a scuffling in the shadows below and a harsh whispering that Helena had to bend down to make out. Rebecca pulled herself through the grate and began to rummage through the drawers.

'Is there any rope in here?' she asked the stranger who stood in the corner mutely. He shook his head, watching as another young woman climbed into his safe room, with a middle-aged woman right behind her.

'There are sheets and stuff though. This is part of the hospital laundry.' He waved a hand to take in the room they stood in.

'That's fine, where are they?'

He walked to a cupboard and opened it, showing piles of freshly laundered towels and sheets. Rebecca pulled a couple down and knotted them together securely. Sam climbed quickly up the ladder to join her at the top. Together they held each end and lowered the centre sling through the hole. Peter and Luke sat a semi-conscious Seth in the sling and supported him carefully as Sam hauled him up. Rebecca had pushed the reluctant stranger beside him, 'volunteering' his assistance in hauling the decommissioned soldier up. Peter climbed the ladder as they pulled, keeping pace at Seth's back, one arm slung over his shoulders to keep him balanced. It didn't take long, though the tedious pace felt like hours as they carefully hoisted their cargo up the tunnel wall. Rebecca and the stranger grabbed Seth's shoulders as they came through the grate and eased him backward onto the concrete floor.

The only sounds in the small room were the heavy pants of exhaustion as they each lay in various heaps. Seth had been left lying near the grate, as no one had the strength to do more than roll a towel to rest his head on and cover him with a sheet. The room was two metres square, one wall crowned with a strip of narrow windows that let in the dimming evening sun. The windows themselves were at street level, suggesting an underground room. One of the doors that led from the room opened onto the large, chemically scented, industrial laundry. Here they managed to find a cart of freshly laundered surgical scrubs, which they changed into, heaping their dirty clothes on the floor. Shadows reached through the high windows; the occasional pair of feet, or what was left of them, scuffed past along the road outside. As they dozed, Helena faintly heard Rebecca's whispered prayer that this would be the last night her family would be separated.

# Chapter Twelve

Jen threw herself back into her work in search of distraction, thankful that she was working in the makeshift mental health division. It was a busy shift, with most of the homeless people who had lived in the tunnels now taking up over half the beds in the area. Some had never seen anyone about their mental health problems and needed close supervision as everyone settled in to the new routine. Jen had been part of the team asked to start the physical examinations and the arduous task suited her need for distraction. Her last patient had just finished showering, a requirement they had insisted on as part of the check-up, and now sat on the chair before her. Lank blonde hair hung around her shoulders and she still had built up dirt around her fingernails. The hot water had reopened a wound in her lower abdomen, a torn patch of skin around the size of her fist. Jen was focused on her other arm though, as down the length of the arm were three clearly defined crescent shaped wounds, all with distinct teeth marks at their edges, all showing bruising more than a day old.

'Dr Marcus, could I see you for a minute?' she called to the doctor who had volunteered to be assigned to the mental health unit for the day. A tall man with a hooked nose and a harried expression came over at her request. Jen quickly explained what she had found. Dr Marcus adopted a pensive look and there was a strange gleam in his eye. His voice lowered as he voiced his thoughts, almost forgetting that Jen was there.

'That makes three now. Three clear attacks that should have resulted in infection. Fifteen people quarantined from bites, all of them have turned within a day.'

Jen watched the distracted doctor pull a notebook from his pocket and flip through it. 'The fever overheats the brain and cooks them. The patient falls into a clinically dead state, then comes back, one, two hours later. Why is this different?' He sounded almost offended that the virus was not behaving in the determined pattern. 'Something in these cases is stopping the infection from taking hold, and in this primitive environment, I can't find the cause!' His voice rose in frustration.

'We did find a few of the infected among the homeless,' Jen put in. The doctor jumped in surprise. *He probably completely forgot I was here*, Jen thought wryly.

'But the infection … is *not* in the mental health rooms.'

He stalked off then, muttering to himself, barking off requests for blood tests to the staff who had come in to assist with the shift. Jen turned back to the scared woman in her own curtained off area, her wide eyes flicking to and fro as she mumbled under her breath. Jen winced at the highly agitated state, but turned to collect the necessary equipment to draw a small vial of blood. The woman's eyes opened even wider as she approached, her dilated pupils locked on the sharp needle in Jen's hand. Deciding not to take the chance, Jen called for a couple of security personnel to hold the woman as she drew the blood. The spooked woman turned feral at their approach, throwing herself off the chair and tucking her hunched figure into a corner, snarling at the men. Lunging together they grabbed her arms, holding her tightly between them. Jen approached warily. She was all too aware of the capabilities of patients in a psychotic state.

She worked quickly, drawing the blood and setting the small vial aside. She took a large step back and motioned for the men holding the frantic woman to let her go. The men released their holds in a practiced motion, each stepping back. The man on her right tripped over the leg of the chair, his hand whipping out to steady himself and grabbing onto the woman's outstretched hand. Jen nearly missed the quick motion as the woman's dirty fingers closed around the grasping hand and pulled him up, sinking her yellowed, chipped teeth into his arm. He screamed, looking shocked at the result of the violent attack. Red welled up in the indents and a small flap of skin peeled back, releasing a stream of blood that streaked down his arm. He turned frightened eyes to Jen, spurring her into action. She grabbed a wad of gauze, pressing it onto the wound.

'Is it … ? Am I … ?' he stuttered.

Jen didn't answer for a minute, not knowing what to say.

'I don't know. She wasn't showing signs of infection, but you'll have to be quarantined. Just in case,' she said softly, biting her lip and looking only at his hand, unable to make eye contact with him. The poor man turned white, clutching his hand to his chest and shaking his head as he backed out of the cordoned off area. Jen didn't follow him; she knew who he was and where he would go. His family was still with the larger group, and she could at least give him a few moments with them.

Her attention turned to the vial of blood in her hand. She sent it with a technician to Dr Marcus and sat heavily at her desk, pulling out a clean book for a new set of patient notes.

*Patient 73: John Campbell*
*Patient Hx: TBD*
*28/12/15 1630hrs*
*Patient was bitten by Patient 61. Broken skin due to bite mark on left hand. Patient appears pale and clammy. Query shock. Patient has temporarily absconded possibly in reaction to the*

*news. Personnel have been sent to bring the patient into quar-
antine. Dr Marcus has been notified and bloods and obs will
be taken when patient presents back to clinic.*

She reviewed the notes, frustrated at the lack of information,
but signed them off anyway. She would have to wait for John to
calm down to finish them.

Dr Marcus flung the curtain aside as he charged once more
into her small area, stepping closely into her personal space as he
did so. 'Where is he?' he demanded brusquely.

'I don't know, he panicked and ran off. He can't go far though,
his family is here, and the tunnels have all been sealed off.'

The imposing man scowled, annoyed at her inability to pro-
duce the patient on request, and sat down in the vacant chair. Her
schizophrenic patient had been moved to a bed in a smaller room
where the other mentally ill quarantined patients were being held.

'I need him here.' Dr Marcus broke the tense silence as he stee-
pled his fingers beneath his sharp nose. 'I need to see both of them
side by side. So far none of our mentally ill patients who have been
attacked have turned. I need to watch the female patient's progress
and see if the virus affects the patient who was bitten and how.'

'John.'

'I'm sorry?'

'The patient's name is John. He's been an orderly in the Royal
Melbourne for eight years. His wife is currently helping in the
kitchens and their three-year-old daughter is running around
in the nursery.' Her voice was sharp, but Dr Marcus didn't look
cowed by the reminder as he returned her gaze unflinchingly.

'It's your job to be the human face in here; I can't afford that
luxury. I see these patients as subjects so that when they turn, and
they will turn, I can do my job and keep this place safe.'

'I understand that, doctor, but these people are scared enough without making it so clinical. If you could at least let the "human faces" do the patient interaction it will make our jobs a lot easier.'

He nodded curtly before standing and sweeping through the curtains. Once he had left, Jen rested her face on the palm of her hand and let exhaustion wash over her.

An orderly was next to interrupt her solitude, flinging the curtains aside violently.

'Jen?' he panted. 'Daniel says he needs to talk you in the comm building urgently.' Message delivered, he walked quickly to where several doctors had gathered around the weak glow of a small tablet in the corner, the nearest they had to a working office at the moment.

Jen walked quickly through the winding corridors to the stairs that served the women's hospital, taking the stairs two at a time. Her breath was laboured as she jogged across the floor to the large desk. Daniel was listening closely to a muted radio, his head bowed low over the desk. His eyes darted up, meeting hers, and he gestured her over.

She could make out the whispered words as she neared the desk. Daniel held up a hand, gesturing for silence.

'They've mentioned a strafing run in two days. They have a couple of people in Geelong doing … something. They haven't said what yet, but it sounds like marking key areas. There was something about a job that took out the train station and a police station, but they said that something they had initially planned wouldn't be adequate. I contacted Joe. He said they're on the way out of Geelong tomorrow afternoon at the latest.' He grinned and handed her the radio next to him. 'And we have a surprise.'

Jen looked puzzled as she took the little black hand-piece. 'Hello?' she said, depressing the mic button.

'Jen!' The familiar happy voice shot through the speaker.

She gripped the desk tightly. 'Sarah?'

# Chapter Thirteen

Karen sat up groggily in the dark room, momentarily disorientated in the unfamiliar surroundings. She could see the prone figures of Rebecca and the boys scattered around the room. The stranger was crouched next to Seth, who had regained consciousness, and they were talking in hushed tones. Helena sat silently nearby, leaning against a bulky laundry bag, shivering slightly in her thin scrubs. Quietly Karen crawled across to them.

'How are you feeling, Seth?' she whispered croakily. The swelling in her throat had been slowly healing, giving her the voice of a long-term smoker and limiting her to restricted sentences only.

He gave her a small smile that looked forced on his pale face. 'I'll cope. Mr Abrahams snuck up to the lower wards and brought back a box of OxyContin so I can move around a little easier now.'

Karen looked down at the leg stretched in front of him. The rough bandaging and crude splint had been replaced with a less restrictive Zimmer splint that almost fully encased his leg.

Seth nodded to the stranger. 'Mr Abrahams here stayed behind to close the doors when everyone was evacuated to the tunnel.' He shot a glance at Rebecca where she lay still with her back to them.

Mr Abrahams took over the telling of the story: 'We managed to evacuate those we could to the tunnel, but the emergency wing was mostly lost. We could only clear the waiting room before the infection spread past the treatment bays.' He stood up and moved to the wall under the strip of windows, looking up at the slow trickle of shambling feet above him. 'The fire doors were already secured and the elevators shut down, so we were fairly sure anyone in the higher levels would be safe. We managed to close the doors to the tunnels from either end. Marie, that's my wife, and I stayed out here so we could secure them all.' He turned his back on the windows, sliding down to sit on the floor. 'She didn't make it. We were cornered outside the emergency wards; she was right behind me. I didn't even think to check the cupboard and, when it swung open, all we saw was a kid. He must have come down from the paediatrics ward and hid before he turned. He still had his dressing gown on.' His voice was distant. 'It was like a nightmare, or a movie. That tiny thing bit into my wife's calf like a mad pup. She never had a chance.' He fell silent, a pained look clouding his face. He rubbed a tired hand across his eyes.

Karen had kept her eyes on Rebecca, whose silent form shook with concealed sobs, but she made no move to join the conversation. Karen turned further around to allow her some level of privacy.

'Did you try to get back to the tunnels?' she asked.

He shook his head. 'The tunnels are on the other side of the emergency rooms,' he explained. 'The doors aren't built to stand up to that kind of assault, so we had to get the ... things ... away from the area completely. It worked as well as we thought. To be honest, I never expected to survive at all. That's why Marie insisted on coming too, despite me begging her to stay in the tunnels.' His voice broke. 'She wasn't meant to be here in the first place. She surprised me with lunch because she didn't want to be alone at work on Boxing Day.' He fell silent, lost in his memories.

Rebecca had settled to the point where she could turn to face them. Her head was still lowered to try to hide her wet, red eyes as she sat up. 'How many made it to the tunnels?'

'Forty.'

'Forty?' she exclaimed angrily, her wide eyes lifting to his. 'All those nurses and doctors, all those patients, and only *forty* got in?' The others stirred as her voice rose.

'Nobody knew what was going on. Reanimated corpses are not the first conclusion one jumps to.' Karen could see he was growing agitated, though he kept his voice steady. 'We did what we could in the panic,' he stated factually as he met her gaze.

Rebecca dropped her eyes again.

He sighed and moved to kneel in front of her. 'Seth told me that you think your family is here, so I understand that this is hard for you, especially with such a low number that made it in. Please understand that I don't say this to get your hopes up, but there is a possibility that they made it in. Or, if not, maybe they managed to escape to one of the other floors before they were sealed off. Survival instincts have been known to drive people to great lengths in terrible situations.'

There was an awkward silence as Rebecca bowed her head. 'I'm sorry, you didn't deserve to wear the brunt of that.' Her head thumped against the wall behind her and he spared her a small grin.

'I think I have a fair idea of what you're going through.'

Rebecca shook her head, wanting to brush off the attempt at comfort.

Sam sat up, blinking the grit from his eyes. 'How do we get to the tunnels? And where do we go from there?' He looked to Seth but it was Mr Abrahams who answered.

'The hospital has been relatively quiet since halfway through day two. I guess the lack of easy food may have sent them elsewhere. I have no idea what's happening upstairs. I haven't been back near the tunnels though, so I'm not sure about that end. I've been sticking to this area. The only other people I've seen were a handful of rough looking characters who broke into the pharmacy about four hours before you guys showed up. I didn't really expect a warm greeting from them so I stayed away. They didn't stay long, just took the drugs they wanted and left. I had to go to the outpatients' wing to get the meds for Seth. I grabbed what I could from the drug room there just in case they came back.' He gestured to the laundry bag under Helena. 'On that note, Seth, it's time for the next dose.'

He pulled out one of the small containers and shook out two tablets into his hand, then passed them to Seth who swallowed them dry.

Helena stood, stretching the kinks from her back as she made her way through to the adjoining laundry room, dragging a laundry bag back with her that was stuffed with long shapes jutting out at awkward angles.

'Two guns with limited ammo will not go very far, so I found something to fill in the gaps till we can find something better.'

The bag fell with a clatter, spilling its contents onto the concrete floor. Helena handed a lighter pair of aluminium crutches to Seth, who was happy to leave the heavier wooden ones behind. Seth pulled himself off the cold floor with a stifled moan. There were several IV poles that had been pulled from their bases that the boys picked up. Karen grabbed a short square table leg, leaving two solid walking sticks for Rebecca and Helena. The shorter woman looked at the stick, which looked comically large in her small hand, and handed it to Mr Abraham.

'I'll stick with the limited ammo. It's a safe bet that you can swing this harder than I can, and you can probably reach the head better too. The best I can hope for is a groin shot, and that's not going to do too much damage.'

Abrahams laughed and took the stick from her.

'Are we going now then?' Sam asked, leaning on the IV pole. Everyone had climbed to their feet and looked to Seth, uncertain of their next move.

'Since we're here already, we'll check the tunnels for any survivors first, then find a way out of Geelong.'

Mr Abrahams glared at Seth. 'I did not lose my wife to those mongrels just to lead them directly to the people we were trying to keep safe!'

'If we leave anyone in there, we're condemning them anyway,' Seth stated softly. 'Do you know where the army reserves base is from here?'

'It's right behind the hospital, just over the road.' Mr Abrahams pointed at the far wall, toward the back of the hospital.

'There's a good chance they have a vehicle of some sort there. We'll head there and get a truck, then get the hell out of the city,' Seth decided, crossing over to the door.

Peter walked up to Seth, his steps hesitant. 'Our sister Meghan is in the Old Gaol. Do you think we could stop there?'

Seth mulled over the idea. 'It is the designated safe house for Geelong. If anyone wants to stay there, they are welcome to. We just need to get through the hospital first. Our paths stay together until then.'

Luke heaved a relieved sigh as he and his twin exchanged glances; they were that much closer to finding the last of their family.

The corridor was quiet as they stepped through, Mr Abrahams taking the lead with Karen and the others close behind. Seth had been pushed into the middle of the group and they kept the pace slow to accommodate him. At the end of the hall, Mr Abrahams moved to the left, eyes darting into every doorway they passed. As they climbed the first staircase, Karen was surprised at the lack of terror she felt as they were once more met with the rolling snarls that preceded the infected.

A *thunk…slide, thunk…slide* echoed down the white corridor. The floor was coated in a grimy brick-red sludge that sucked at their dirty wet shoes as they stepped across it. They took their posts at either side of the staircase as the rest of the group joined them.

Rebecca sucked in a panicked gasp as shadows reached across the far end of the hall. She turned to alert the others only to see three of the infected already making their way toward the group from behind. The *thunk…slide* was joined by a chorus of sucking steps as, one by one, seven creatures joined the party, cutting the corridor off completely.

'Oh shit, now what?' Sam cried, his pole at his shoulder as he turned wildly, trying to face both sides at once.

Rebecca ran to the door opposite, opening it onto a tiny, office-style exam room. She closed it quickly, seeing no door or windows in the room, and moved to the next door. The layout was the same; however, this room had a door in the opposite wall. Seeing no other option, she frantically beckoned them all through, slamming the door shut as the first of the creatures reached them. Karen already had the other door open, revealing a narrow storeroom with a door at the far end. Mr Abrahams took the lead once more.

'This leads to the maintenance corridors. They run behind the old exam rooms and meet up with the main floor this side of the new emergency rooms. The renovations haven't gotten this far yet.' He nudged the door open slowly, waiting almost a full minute to be sure there weren't any hidden dangers. The lack of noise had him pushing the door open fully and waving them through.

As Seth brought up the rear into the small corridor, Abrahams closed the door and yelled in shock; a slight, stringy haired creature had been hidden by the open door, her throat and vocal cords were long gone, either torn or ripped out violently, leaving her with a sub-audible hiss instead of the loud growled warning they had become used to. She snatched at his shirt, bringing his face toward her mouth. Seth swung a crutch at her head, pushing his weight to the side of the narrow space as Sam and Peter tried to get through to help. Abrahams pushed hard at the skinny grey figure, her fingernails tearing at the soft skin of his throat as she fought to keep hold of her victim.

In his attempt to escape her grip, Abrahams twisted his foot beneath him, dropping him to his knees. The hooked fingers of the creature finally found purchase in his skin and tore at the tissue as she followed him down, landing on top of her squirming prey. She opened her mouth, stained teeth descending on the vulnerable neck bared beneath her. A hard thump across the back of her neck drove her teeth into the flesh and she ripped upwards, dark blood spurting across the corridor.

Sam looked horrified as he stood, pole raised above his head, coated from head to toe with hot arterial spray. The gory head looked up, distracted from the twitching flesh beneath her by the uninfected group. As she started to pull herself up, her milky eyes fixed on Sam, Peter stepped up, driving the hollow point of the IV pole into her skull and through Mr Abrahams' chest below. Her legs flattened out behind her and she fell over her victim.

'I killed him,' Sam said softly.

Karen pushed through the stunned group to his side, her protective instincts taking over. She clasped his head to her shoulder as she physically turned his face away.

'You tried to stop her.' She pulled his head up to face her. 'Don't do this. There are going to be many more times from here on that you'll have to do things, either accidentally or on purpose, that will be worse than this, and you cannot let it get to you. If you do, that's it. You die - those around you die. Do you understand me?'

He nodded jerkily into her shoulder, blood smearing her hospital clothes. Seth pulled himself up onto his crutches, hobbling away from the stained walkway.

'Let's keep moving. The sooner we're away, the better,' he tossed over his shoulder.

Karen forced the pale boy in front of her and they made their way silently to the far door. The thin plywood doors had been chained shut, the workmen evidently relying on the security of the hospital's inner courtyard to keep the area secure. Seth easily pulled the IV pole from Sam's hand and wedged it behind the chain, twisting it down firmly to try breaking through the wooden doors. Seth stumbled, hopping on his poor leg as he slipped. Luke moved up beside him, pushing him gently to the side before taking his place. With the solid base offered by two feet, the tightened chain slowly sawed through the thin wood, releasing the chain completely. Luke pulled the chain free with a rattle, wrapping the metal links around his wrist. He pushed the doors open onto a ruined reception area, the plastic sheets and abandoned workhorses speaking of tradies who would never meet their completion date. Luke pushed through the translucent curtains ahead of the group, jumping every time something moved in the corner of his eye. He led the silent group through to the far wall, shifting through the curtains to find the door hidden behind the layers. He pushed the door in on silent hinges.

The room was dark, the emergency lights alone providing a dim guide across the crowded workspace. The floor was still sticky underfoot and they could barely make out the dark smeared tracks against the pale floor. Karen eyed the floors distastefully, happy for the lack of light. Sam still stood silent and pale and Karen was worried the young man might be in shock, but they had no time to address it now.

Helena cursed softly as she stumbled over a black lump in the dark, her short legs unable to make the long strides that the others made easily. A soft moan rising from the floor turned her blood to ice and she froze, eyes glued to Rebecca, who had turned frightened eyes toward the noise. The lump twitched behind the short woman and she danced away from the prone figure, colliding with Seth as she did so. He wobbled, catching his balance on his crutches, and shot her a confused glare. Wordlessly she pointed at the figure that had raised its milky gaze in their direction at the suggestion of fresh prey, extending a hand toward its meal. Seth pushed her through to the rest of the group and the thing snarled as its prey moved out of reach and tried to pull its ruined body toward them. An answering growl sounded to their right, and another figure hobbled toward them, the few dim lights throwing his face into contorted shadows.

Rebecca stifled a sob, her hand flying up to cover her mouth as she stared at the drooling figure that made its way toward her, arms outstretched.

'Ben!' she sobbed. The figure kept approaching with no sign of recognition of his sister.

Seth's eyes widened and he waved the group on quickly. 'Luke, Karen and Helena, take Sam and Rebecca and move, now! Peter, I need you to stay back please.' Karen and Helena ushered the other two away. Rebecca screamed and hit out at Karen, fighting to stay. Luke grabbed her other arm, dragging her away physically from her infected brother.

'Now,' Seth said softly, looking to the corner where the others had vanished. Luke raised his pole like a spear and drove the end into Ben's milky eye, right through the skull. He froze and dropped to the floor with a soft thump. Luke turned and did the same to the zombie that was still pulling its useless legs along the floor toward them, driving the pole down until it hit the floor.

Luke and Seth were silent as they joined the others in front of the fire doors that closed off the tunnels. A chain, similar to the one that covered Luke's wrist, secured the doors tightly. Helena held a sobbing Rebecca where she was crouched on the ground; Sam had snapped out of his stupor and now stared through the small window in the centre of one door, a look of horror on his face.

'Now what?' Seth muttered to himself, hobbling to the window on the second door.

Bodies covered the floor within the tunnel, most of them moving sluggishly, some quicker, eyes honing in on the change of light and movement in the windows and moving closer to the doors with their drunken gait. If Rebecca's parents had been in the tunnel, someone had locked the virus in with them. Wanting nothing more than to leave the bloody hospital, Seth pushed them on.

Rebecca trailed the group to the back of the hospital, lost in her thoughts. They took a careful half hour to complete the normally ten-minute walk. Helena led them through the familiar halls, ducking into service rooms to avoid the main floors and corridors that seemed to tremble under the distant growls and stumbling steps of the dead. Helena moved ahead like a silent shadow, using gestures and pointed looks to communicate. Seth limped along on his crutches behind her, grabbing her shoulder if he heard something she had missed, or if something caught his eye. He left the boys to keep an eye on Rebecca where she kept dropping behind. He was proud of how they kept herding her forward to the safety of the group, simultaneously keeping a silent watch on their surroundings.

Helena hesitated before opening the door in front of her.

'Is something wrong?' Seth asked her, leaning down heavily on his crutches.

'So far, the hospital has been overrun by these things.' She seemed hesitant. Seth remained silent, allowing her to go at her own pace. 'This is the only way to exit the hospital on this side, and the army reserve base is straight over the road from the main door.' She threw a glance back to Rebecca. 'But this is the maternity and NICU wing.'

Seth understood her reluctance now. If the infection had made it this far and managed to bypass the security doors, they were potentially walking into an ugly scene. He nudged the door open a fraction, taking in the gore-covered floor in front of the reception desk and the torn arm that had caught between the security door opposite, wedging it slightly open. He shuddered as he heard the few soft, whispering moans trickle through the open door. He could clearly see the automatic doors at the end of the final corridor leading to the road.

He nodded to Helena to open the door slowly, hoping she would be able to keep her composure, and hung back, waiting for the boys to draw closer.

'Don't look through the door. Our only goal at the moment is to get through without stopping or breaking down completely.'

Sam looked confused, trying to see what had their leader spooked. Seth put a firm hand on his head, pulling his attention back. The young man nodded and moved to Rebecca's side. She stood in shock still, her pale face pointed at the floor, shaking slightly. Sam took her arm and steered her through the maintenance door.

Helena couldn't resist darting a look at the propped open door where the soft, whining growls escaped the tiny occupants that she knew would be beyond the open door. She could see brown stains on the soft baby blue carpet and covering the cartoon characters that grinned down from the walls. A heavy thump and the movement of a slow shadow behind the heavy door pushed her short legs into a faster walk. Eager to move on, she could hear quick steps and the creak of Seth's crutches as they kept easy pace with her tiny steps. She released a stuttering breath as the automatic doors leading out of the building slid open at her approach.

Slipping through and moving to the right, Helena pressed her small frame against the wall to wait for the others to join her at the top of the sloping path, all wearing expressions of relief to be free of the massive mausoleum. Cars lined the narrow street between the hospital and the reserves base, and the fence that blocked the area off from the street. The grey box of the gaol beside it cast a shadow over the yard. The front door hung open, and at least three bodies were piled up around the entrance.

'I'm sorry,' Seth said simply.

Luke leant heavily into his twin's side, a lost and gutted look on his face.

Seth reached out and plucked the walking stick from Rebecca's numb fingers. 'I don't suppose anyone here can hotwire a car?' he asked, half-jokingly.

Sam sheepishly raised a hand. 'I got the job at the train station as part of my community service. I don't suppose I can get in trouble for it now though.'

Seth grinned at this first bit of good luck and looked at the car choices in front of him. As tempting as it might be to just grab one of these cars and flee, he knew there had been an exercise involving the Bushmaster military vehicles in this region within the last month, and if there was a chance that those beasts were still hiding in the sheds, he wanted to take the chance to drive it out. He pointed out a grey sedan that was reverse parked in front of the base.

'I could do it in my sleep,' said Sam.

Seth handed the walking stick to him. 'Can you do it with that thing breathing down your neck?'

He pointed to the pale, stocky figure that hobbled toward them in a baby-doll nightie, his short blonde hair patched with dried blood. The left arm had been torn off completely, so the skimpy lingerie hung loose off a shoulder, exposing half of a solid, hairy chest. Sam had no idea whether to burst out laughing or shrink in horror, settling for a strangled laugh instead.

Peter stepped up beside him, saying, 'I'll watch your back.'

Sam smiled in thanks, unable to look away from the lace-clad figure. He turned to Seth again. 'After we break in, do you want us to drive up here?'

Seth shook his head. 'You won't get up here with the cars in the way,' he pointed out. 'Just drive the car through the chain link fence. We'll move as close as we can and follow you in. Hopefully we'll be quick enough to avoid *Baby-doll* and his mates. Head for the garages once you're in.' He pointed to the large sheds in the yard.

Sam nodded, shooting a nervous glance at the disturbing group, then dashed down the slight incline to the old sedan. Peter followed, hot on his heels.

Sam drove the crook of the walking stick into the window, sending glass shards raining onto the black tar. No alarm gave him away, but the loud crash was enough to spur on the growling group and, as one, they turned and headed for the hidden duo.

Peter stayed behind Sam while he curled his torso under the wheel and stripped the wires.

'Get in quickly.' Sam's muffled voice tumbled out and Peter threw himself in, hearing a rapid sparking before the rough engine roared to life. Peter buckled his seatbelt as Sam shifted the car into gear, grinding the gears with an awful crunch. The car leapt onto the curb and barrelled into the wire-topped fence, fishtailing in front of the garage. Peter leapt out as Sam brought the car around to face the three tall roller-doors.

A glance behind showed Seth was barely ahead of the reach of the macabre group, with Helena running as fast as she could to keep up with the rest. Luke had managed to rally, and ran beside them, swinging and spearing his IV pole to keep the creatures at bay. Rebecca and Karen crossed the fence line. The younger woman had seemingly taken courage from Luke's reaction and now ran with purpose, pausing to pull up the side of the fence as Helena and Seth drew near.

Sam stomped hard on the accelerator, spinning the wheels on the dirt road. The car lurched forward, tyres kicking up dust before the car ploughed into the last thin corrugated sheet of the shed door, bending it severely in the middle and knocking it free of its tracks. Sam threw the car into reverse, backing out of the cavernous room into the sinking afternoon sun. As he cleared the twisted frame, Karen and Rebecca slipped into the darkness, the others following them through.

Baby-doll was still following their movement in the fading light and had reached the uprooted fence. A shape loomed out at them from the dark interior and Seth almost collapsed in relief as he recognised the long boxy shapes of two Bushmaster troop movers he had hoped would be there. He herded his small group toward the huge shape and climbed in through the unlocked door.

Once the doors were closed, Seth sighed in relief and stretched out on three of the rear seats that lined the solid walls, his leg throbbing beneath him. The others collapsed into the seats around him.

'Has anyone driven a van before?' he asked.

'I have a four-wheel drive at home …' Karen offered uncertainly as the others shook their heads. Seth cocked an eyebrow at Karen. 'I'm fine to drive,' she insisted.

Seth frowned but began to explain how the vehicle worked. 'It's close enough. This has a push button start but drives similarly.' He stressed *similarly*, in case the new features threw Karen off, or she figured out that this had nothing in common with her family car. She climbed into the higher seat, with Rebecca slipping into the passenger seat beside her and the boys from the car clambering up into the cavernous back.

Baby-doll had pushed through the fence and made it to the ruined door, stepping into the deeper shadows. The silhouette draped by the sheer fabric looked ridiculous on the army base.

'What the hell is that?' Rebecca asked, staring at the bizarre sight.

Karen pushed the small button below the wheel, the powerful engine purring to life below her. She pushed the heavy truck into gear and moved forward, barely flinching as another door fell before them. She manoeuvred the heavy truck through the first hole in the chain fence. The wheels caught one of the creatures, dragging it to the ground, and took out two more when they crowded in close before all wheels could touch the tar of the main road. Rebecca put her head down in her hands and let a sob slip out as they finally headed away from the ravaged city.

# Chapter Fourteen

Joe moved slowly through the radio channels in the quiet house. Daniel had just signed off after warning them about the threat headed their way. He was scanning the radio for the channel Daniel had told them to look for without luck. They had already checked with some of their shared contact to see if anyone had heard anything more, but they knew as little as Joe did. Sarina had been able to fill them in a little about the fate of the Bellarine area though.

She had told them how the army had cordoned off the highway that led to the Queenscliff fort, denying entry to the thousands of people who had tried to crowd into the narrow strip, including Sarina and her family. They had been forced to run as several people in the crowd around them succumbed to infected bites and turned on their friends and neighbours, throwing the massing crowd into a screaming panic. Sarina had narrowly avoided the frantic fingers of a screaming, overweight woman who had a young man's teeth buried in her meaty throat and his fingers tangled through her loose hair. Sarina had managed to gather together what remained of her small family and run to Point Henry, where they had slept in shifts in the deserted Alcoa car park. Her son Alex had been the first to slide into the driver's seat and flick through the radio channels, finding first Daniel, then Joe, who had encouraged them to forage what they could from the cars and trucks around them. Alex had also found Ian on the radio, a local fisherman who had been happy to take advantage of the family's desperate plight to offer them passage to Tasmania—which he had insisted remained untouched—for the cost of half their gathered food and weapons. They had agreed, setting aside what they could hide under their clothes before arranging the meeting at the end of the long pier that speared out into the ocean from their small beach.

Before they had left, Sarina had told Joe and Daniel what they had planned, falling back on ingrained behaviour of alerting someone to their plans before they climbed onto the dilapidated ship late on day three. They only contacted Daniel once more after that, calling from the ship to report the crowded refugee tents sprawled across the Swan Island defence force base off the Queenscliff coast, and the small planes, boats and ships of all sizes that looked like they were evacuating the base under the disciplined eye of the military. Sarina had also managed to describe the massing hordes of infected that could be seen swarming along the formerly picturesque coast. Before signing off she had promised to try to make contact when—*if*—they reached safety.

A small book sat beside Joe's hand with a short list of names written in Anica's neat print. 'Daniel' and 'Melbourne' made up the first line, along with the channel on which they had been communicating. 'Sean' and 'Werribee' came next with their channel, but this had already been crossed out and 'taken? dead?' was scribbled in the margin beside it. 'Blue' and 'Ballarat' were on the next line, with 'taken? Grampians?' written in the margin. Joe had made a note to keep trying the channel though, in case Blue had survived the escape and found a way to make contact from the mountains.

Joe looked at the last name on the list and put a line through 'Sarina' and 'Queenscliff', scribbling 'taken? Tasmania?' into the margin. He turned in his chair to stretch his spine, glancing over at the others in the room.

When James could be persuaded to take some rest, he entrusted Charlie to his parents, who were happy to have their granddaughter to focus on. The day that Joe had made contact with Melbourne, and Daniel had told the group about the threat posed, James's worries had grown, until nothing could distract him from his dark thoughts.

Sarah had already spoken with Joe about her concerns. Both of them agreed that James would soon lose patience and want to go after his wife to bring her back to safety. They had concluded that, when the time came, one of them would go with him.

It was late on day four when Sarah heard the screen door being pushed open softly. She glanced over at Joe, who was still awake after his watch, and he nodded at her, taking her seat to relieve her watch as she went after her brother. She wasted no time in following him out into the warm evening. James had started to scale the huge gate heading to his small car parked along the street. Quickening her steps, she grabbed his arm and hauled him back into the driveway to the ute, opening the passenger door to shove him in. She grabbed the key from where it rested in the letterbox and unchained the gate before jumping in and coasting silently down the driveway. She walked back to relock the heavy chain, pushing the key into the mailbox again.

James shot her a dark look.

'If you insist on this foolish idea, at least take the car with the bloody radio,' she said as she slid into the driver's seat again. They drove in silence for a while, Sarah knowing where he had intended to go, moving toward the city automatically.

'Why?' he asked after a while, eyes fixed on the road ahead at the point where it disappeared beneath them.

'Because you're an idiot,' she replied. 'Because you don't know how to drive a manual. Because I care about her too, and you taking off and getting yourself killed because you're not thinking straight is going to kill our parents.' She glared out into the darkness, not looking over at him, though she could feel his eyes as they shifted to her.

A frantic knocking on the rear window had her yanking the car violently to the side, fishtailing as she fought to regain control before slamming on the breaks and stopping near the side of the road. Her hands shook where they were glued to the wheel and she panted heavily through her fright.

'What the hell are you doing back there?' she hissed as a shaken Nell slid out of the ute tray. James shuffled unhappily into the middle seat to make room for her.

'I was supposed to be on watch,' Nell explained quietly, still shaky as she tried to regain composure. 'And James said I should stay here because it had better coverage.'

'I thought we agreed she wasn't allowed to be in charge of our safety,' Sarah muttered in an aside to James.

He just shrugged sheepishly. 'It was a joke. I knew you were on watch. I didn't think she'd actually do it!'

Sarah growled at him, and pulled slowly onto the road again. She took the small roads where she could, pulling the hardy off-road ute onto the footpaths when cars and packs of the infected blocked the road completely. They had to change direction several times, forging their path toward the city silently; parts of the distant skyline were still shrouded in a light smoke as unseen fires smouldered. Every road they turned down was swarmed by more of the vaguely human creatures, which grabbed at the vehicle as they passed. They tried their best to ignore them, but the occasional thumps under their wheels still had them cringing in disgust.

The radio squawked to life in the dashboard, startling a squeal from Nell. James grabbed the mouthpiece.

'We're here.'

'Well, you're certainly not *here*.' Joe's gruff voice sounded pissed off even through the distortion of the radio. 'David called back. The package we're waiting for is on its way to the city now, so *hurry up*.' He bit the words out sharply before clicking off without a sign off.

James replaced the receiver and hid his face against his hand. 'We're out of time,' he said unnecessarily, before shooting a pleading look at Sarah.

She growled and grabbed at the mouthpiece. 'Pack everything and everyone up and head out of town. Just clear the house and move off to … Meredith.' She was grasping at straws, calling out the name of the tiny town that she knew for sure would be out of the blast range. The fact that it was on the way to their planned destination helped in her spontaneous decision.

Joe was quick to respond. 'Roger that. Your parents have already started reorganising the cars. Could have used the ute though.'

Sarah didn't bother with a reply. Her focus was set on the choked up freeway in front of her. 'Of course it's blocked,' she chastised herself aloud. 'Two hundred thousand people gagging to leave on a two-lane highway. Do the math idiot!'

They had pulled up on the footpath opposite a small bluestone church, their circuitous route pushing them past the city and onto the hill parallel to the hospital. Sarah was still edgy about Nell's sudden appearance, and the constant growls and shadows they had passed as they drove had her nerves stretched tight. Even now as they paused, she could make out the shadows moving among the graveyard of cars. James looked gutted as he searched anxiously for any break between the cars that they might fit through.

The line of cars stretched the length of the road. Some had tried to cross to the other side of the road, but the confusion had resulted in a metal tangle of twisted cars blocking access to the other side as well. The forest of trucks, cars and other people movers looked black in the evening sky and they could only just make out the shadows passing through the gaps. Closer to their position, the shadows stretched into barely recognisable human figures, some looking less human than others, all sporting injuries and disfigurements of various severity. The guttural growls and snarls washed over them, almost shaking the windows with their rumbling force.

Sarah decided to back up and try another route. She threw the ute into reverse and looked to check over her shoulder when James rested his hand on hers.

'Wait. Can you hear that?' he asked, his voice hushed and head cocked to the side.

Sarah and Nell seemed to hear it at the same time. Sarah wound the window down a crack to listen more closely. A heavy rumbling cut through the noisy twilight, the steadiness setting it apart from the fluctuating growls. Nell saw it first, her finger pointing at the lumbering shadow that crept out of the darkness of the street beside the church. Sarah wavered her hand over the headlight switch, undecided as to whether she should make her presence known. The door to the truck opened and a figure in nondescript baggy clothes leaned through an open window, copying James's previous action of scanning the streets for a break.

Suddenly James let out a strangled yell and bolted out the door.

'JAMES!' Nell screamed, sliding into his seat, arm stretched out as if to stop him.

Sarah sat in shocked silence as she watched the dark figure dart between the parked cars. The growling turned menacing as the noise and frantic movement attracted the nearest zombies. Sarah was slow to react when Nell jumped out the open door as the hungry figures honed in on James's dark figure, where he hopped over part of a car in the middle of the road.

'Nell, don't you fucking dare! Get back in the bloody car!' she screamed, throwing her own door open. The creatures that had been drawn to James's mad dash now turned toward the nearer food source, the growling reaching an almost deafening level. The road seemed to shake as Sarah watched Nell cross the first line of cars. She screamed as a zombie clasped its greedy hands around Nell's wrist and pulled it up to a gaping mouth. Sarah grabbed the steering lock from the foot well on the passenger side and darted out after her.

Out of the corner of her eye, she thought she could see that James had made it to the truck and was holding the blonde pyjama-clad figure close, but she brushed it aside, focusing on Nell's writhing figure as she fought the zombie's hold.

Something big and black teased at Sarah's peripheral vision. A huge plane was flying just over the bay. She broke into a run as a second figure reached for Nell's other arm; she could hear her friend's frightened sobs and choked off screams as she drew close enough to bring the heavy wheel lock down on the head of the first creature, allowing Nell to pull her arm free. Sarah swung out at the second zombie, the blow glancing off its arm and spinning it around.

Rebecca screamed from where she was held tightly in James's arms. She had watched her husband make a suicide run across the blocked highway, her heart leaping into her mouth when she had finally recognised his face. Another figure had dashed after him, screaming his name before being yanked backward by one of the silhouettes. She thought she saw Sarah, wielding only a thin bar, running after her. Rebecca watched in horror as her sister-in-law took down one zombie, wheeling on the second. She screamed when she saw a third shadow move in from behind. James's arms tightened around her in distress as he took in the scene. Rebecca could feel his quick breath panting against her back.

The third figure snatched Nell's recently freed arm, yanking it to the side and sinking its teeth into her neck. Her shriek of horror and pain was cut off in a burbling cough; the black spray that stood out starkly against the dark orange sky stopped, and she fell limp into the dead arms.

Sarah cried out wordlessly as Nell stopped moving. She almost didn't notice as the second creature struggled to its feet beside her, but she swung down hard, cleaving its skull under the weighty bar. Nell's limp body was dropped as the last creature clawed at Sarah's back, dragging her violently to the ground where she was hidden from view by the cars. Her cries went silent.

James stared numbly at the swarming shadows, as more and more crowded to the spot where he had last seen his sister. He wanted to run over and beat them off her; he wanted to see her fight her way out from under the predators, but he couldn't move. Peter climbed out from the back of the army truck and approached them quickly.

'I really sorry, but we have to go.' He took hold of James's arm, Rebecca held onto the other, and they tugged him backward. A sharp whistle cut through the thick growls.

James put up a weak protest, pulling his arm away from the unknown boy, but they held on and guided his resisting body back to the army truck, pushing him into the last seat. As they backed the truck up and pulled onto the footpath, heading away from the town, there was earthshaking *boom* and the tiny rear window turned a blinding white as the shockwave of an explosion pushed the truck forward, clipping a small tree and leaving them stalled beside the graveyard of cars.

They sat in stunned silence, most of them clueless as to what had caused the explosion. James kept his head down and wept.

# Chapter Fifteen

Seth winced as Karen steered the cumbersome truck down the crowded footpaths, clipping cars and poles as she tried to avoid the bigger pileups. She found a small gap between the wreckage that allowed them to pass, and drove, keeping the nose of the truck pointed away from the burning city. The explosion that had stalled them in the road left them all temporarily stunned, the cherry red glow of fire stretching out in the distance behind them. He suspected that James had an idea of what caused the explosion but left him to his grief for the time being.

After twenty minutes of aimless driving he cleared his throat. 'I don't want to be the heartless bastard, but we need to know where we're headed. We don't want to be heading away from where we need to be.'

James lifted his head slowly. 'Meredith.'

'Who?' Seth looked confused.

'It's a town out past Geelong.' Karen glanced over her shoulder briefly as she spoke. 'I know it; my house is out that way.'

They drove in silence. Rebecca was grateful for the lack of windows, not wishing to see the source of the snarls and intermittent thumps along the side or under the armoured truck. James refused to tear his eyes from the floor, focusing on the rivets under his feet. As the truck forged its way through the congested roads, Helena could see Seth's face draining of colour, a thin sheen of sweat starting to bead on his brow. She pulled the pillowcase from under her feet and reached in, pulling out the small strip of tablets that Mr Abrahams had used at the hospital. She handed them over to Seth who took them without complaint, swallowing them dry once more.

The truck pulled over without warning and Karen turned to look back at the tense group.

'What's wrong?' Rebecca asked, as she moved to shift her husband's head from her shoulder.

Karen waved her back. 'Nothing's wrong. This is the first petrol station I've gone past that looks empty and has all its windows intact.' She stood from her seat and made her way through the forest of legs to the rear door.

Seth jerked his head at Luke and the young man shot to his feet with his IV pole in hand, his twin close behind. Seth grabbed the pole as he passed, handing him the small gun instead.

Luke hesitated. 'I've never shot a real gun before,' he said quietly.

'Safety, point, shoot. Keep your finger *off* the trigger unless you intend to shoot.' Seth pointed out the safety, then looked at him with firm eyes. 'Only if you have to.' He waited for the young man to nod before releasing the barrel.

Karen spared them a glance before pushing the door open and hopping onto the hard ground, the wary boys close behind. Seth and Sam hopped down after them, Seth taking point as Sam started to fill the fuel tank.

The petrol station was a one-pump stop with the rusted carcasses of cars standing tall against the night sky. They walked softly as they made their way to the old boxy building, squinting as their eyes adjusted to the darkness. They couldn't resist taking in deep breaths as they enjoyed the sudden stillness in the clean air they had taken for granted barely five days ago. As their approach seemed to offer no new dangers, Karen and the twins grew bolder, walking a little faster on the dry grass, their backs losing a little of the tension that continued to plague them all.

Luke reached the door first and pushed the handle. The locked door caught them by surprise, having so far met only doors left unlocked in the panic. He gave a quick look to his twin before shrugging and butting the end of the pole into the window. They cringed at the loud crash, crouching into the deeper shadow of the wall and listening closely. When no growls met them, Luke stood again and reached into the broken window, finding the lock and releasing it. The door swung open easily this time, sounding a small bell that ran through the room. Karen walked to the tiny fridge and started scooping water bottles into her arms as Luke and Peter moved to the confectionery stand, piling nuts and chocolates into their shirts.

A snick behind them had them freezing in their action.

'And just what are you doing with our food?' A soft voice curled around their ears. 'Turn around love, let's see what you found.'

Assuming a boldness she didn't feel, Karen turned slowly and looked at the looming figure that stood between her and the door. She could see the gun in his hand, the slight sheen reflecting in what little light managed to penetrate the grimy window.

'I'm sorry, we didn't know this place was still operational. We can pay if you like.'

The shadow huffed. 'Pay?' He laughed. 'With what?'

Karen shivered as his eyes raked down her body.

'Even if you did happen to have your purse squirrelled away in those pants, I doubt the banks will be opening any time soon. And this place is *not* operational. That's why the door was locked.'

Karen glanced at the door. It was still ajar behind the stranger and she was sure she could reach it, but the boys were on the other side of the room. There was no way they would be able to get past. The man moved slightly further into the light; his face remained deeply in the shadow but now she could see his vest clearly. Her heart sunk at the bright yellow sneer of a hornet sitting proudly on his chest.

The biker smirked as he saw the recognition bloom in her eyes; he waved the gun to the side, gesturing to the floor below the window.

'Sit,' he said calmly.

Luke was closest to the window and crouched without a word. His gaze swept the floor, looking for a way out. Peter was right behind him, tucking himself into a ball. Karen was slower, still holding onto the bottles of water. The Frenzy member seemed to grow impatient, kicking at her knee to push her down. She cried out in pain, the bottles rolling out of her hands and across the floor. The barrel of the gun lowered toward her.

'I'm truly sorry about this, but you understand that I can't let you take our supplies. You can, however, consider yourself lucky that I'm the only one here. An hour earlier and the others would have been very happy to keep you around a little longer,' he said silkily, looking meaningfully at her and then the boys. 'All of you.'

'I'm sorry,' Karen panted out. 'Please let us go. We just wanted to rest … we can find somewhere else!' Her head came up, pleading with him. He knelt down before her, gun still levelled at her nose.

'I think you'll find that my way leaves no loose ends. Consider this a mercy. I am releasing you from this hell on earth to find your rewards beyond.' He gestured widely with his arms; the light slanting across his face showed his smirk as he spoke. His finger moved to the trigger and Karen screwed her face up tight in the face of the cold barrel.

Luke gave a cry and threw his weight into the stomach of the vested biker. The report of the gun deafened them in the small room before the metal could be heard skittering across the floor.

Karen fell sideways, cradling her ears, and Peter grabbed her arm and pulled her to her feet. Luke spared a look at the gun in the corner, deciding against going for it when the large man found his feet surprisingly quickly.

The three jerked a staggered path outside to the armoured car on the side of the road, ducking low when three rapid shots peppered the ground ahead of them. James flung open the rear door and they threw themselves onto the floor inside, panting heavily. He pulled the heavy door shut, peering into the darkness outside the tiny window.

'Where are you hit?' Peter's voice was frantic as he pulled at Karen's hands where they grabbed at her left side.

'I wasn't hit!' she protested, pulling her hands back.

'Bullshit, what's that?' He was almost shouting, pointing at the dark patch that seeped through her overalls.

'It's a scratch, trust me. If I was hit, you'd know about it!' She struggled to her feet, moving to the front of the truck.

'Where the hell do you think you're going?' Peter yelled, trying to block her path. Karen glared at him as she ripped at the hole in the fabric, showing him the superficial graze that wept blood onto her white clothes.

'Now, if you're finished checking me out, can I get back in the truck and get us the hell out of here?' She didn't wait for an answer, turning briskly and swivelling herself into the driver's seat with the barest of winces.

Shots pinged against the truck as the powerful engine roared to life and accelerated down the dark road. Karen peered into the darkness blindly, unwilling to turn on the headlights and draw more attention than they had already attracted. She tried to ignore the sharp ricochets of the bullets against the truck's iron skin. Finally deciding that she preferred a quick getaway over a clean one, she flicked the headlights on. They illuminated the road ahead and she gasped in horror, pulling everyone's attention away from the man standing in the centre of the road behind them, muzzle flashes highlighting his face with each shot.

Two lines of infected people struggled to move on either side of the road, though none seemed to be getting any closer. In shock, Karen had slowed the truck to a crawl and the sporadic gunfire stopped behind them.

'Maybe he ran out of bullets,' Peter mused.

A heavy-set brunette was nearly level with the nose of the truck and seemed to be turning on a wooden peg leg. Karen gagged when she realised what she was actually seeing. A tall spike had been forced through her centre so the sharp tip protruded through the back of her neck, pulling her collared shirt tight against the front of her throat. Her right leg was missing below the hem of her skirt, leaving her twisting around the stake aimlessly, arms reaching for the light ahead of her. Karen understood now why none of them had approached the truck. Each had been secured to the ground in a similar manner. The macabre trophies eagerly pawed at the air in front of them.

A thick throaty chuckle alerted them to the tall figure that had caught up to the stalled truck and stepped in front of them, throwing his face into the light. His eyes were a muddy brown under his thick mess of blonde hair and he followed their gaze to the bloody scarecrows before looking back at them and sneering.

'Don't worry, I can always make room for more.'

He levelled the gun at Karen through the windscreen. She pushed down on the accelerator and the truck leapt forward, forcing him to jump to the side. They sped off, eager to leave the rows of dead behind them.

After fifteen minutes of terrifying speed through the dark winding roads, Karen made a turn into a rough side street, sending up plumes of dust on either side, and pulled over again.

'You're not stopping for water again are you? It didn't work out so well last time,' Peter said.

'No, but I can't keep driving. If I don't stop for a break, the next place I park this thing in will be a tree.' She rested her head on her hands where they still gripped the steering wheel tightly.

'We could all do with some rest,' Seth pointed out. They had been dozing on and off since their rest in the hospital laundry, and in the aftermath of the adrenaline rush, their exhaustion was starting to show in their drawn out silences. They lay close to conserve warmth, stretching onto the narrow floor between the seats, and fell into a fitful rest.

They slept longer than they thought they would, exhaustion keeping them down until the morning sun streamed in through the small window in the back, warming them slowly. Seth woke first, snapped out of his rest by a throbbing ache that pulled at his leg. He swallowed two of the small pills before slipping out of the truck to relieve himself, less quietly than he hoped with the clumsy splint and the crutches under his arms. He soon heard movement behind him as the others woke and walked out into the morning sun to stretch. Karen had somehow managed to pull the car over behind a rustic home nearly swallowed up by the trees around it, the lush greenery and neat gardens making the carnage in Geelong seem like a distant nightmare.

Karen disappeared behind the truck, ostensibly for the same reason as Seth, and Rebecca and James stretched out on the grass. This left the boys alone in the Bushmaster to examine the truck more closely than they had been able to during their rushed escape.

Seth had just zipped up when two cries reached him. One echoed from inside the truck while the other clearly came from Karen on the other side. She tripped over herself as she came around the open rear door, nearly falling into Sam as he jumped down the step in front of her. There was an unintelligible garble as the two of them spoke over each other. They both stopped, looking at one another.

'Ladies first,' he gestured.

'Good news and bad news,' she began. 'Good news is we accidentally found Meredith in the dark; the bad news is the infection found it first. The street is impassable just past the trees. It was pure luck that I stopped on this side last night, or they would have been all over us this morning!'

'Well, I found—'

'*We* found ...' Peter and Luke hopped down to join them on the ground.

'We found weapons!' they said in unison. Seth looked sceptical.

'Really? Soldiers don't leave firearms in trucks.'

'Not firearms—these!' Peter excitedly held out a multi-tool and a wicked looking fixed blade knife. 'There's heaps in the locker at the back!'

Seth took the knife and smiled. 'This is a Phobius M9 Bayonet,' he said. 'How many of these are there?'

'Ten of each.' Sam pulled out another from his belt.

Karen frowned and picked up the multi-tool, examining it to keep from doing anything rash, such as confiscating the sharp blades from the young men. 'This won't be enough to take on a horde.'

'It's better than these.' Seth held up a crutch. 'And we have about five bullets between both handguns. We're not going to be taking them on; we just want to get past safely.'

'Can't we just drive over them like we did before?' Karen asked.

He shook his head. 'As awesome as this thing is, there is actually a limit to how many people you can run over without stuffing the engine. I'm not eager to find out what the exact number is.'

Seth pulled himself back up into the truck, swinging his leg up into the next seats to make room for the others to file past. 'You said you live around here,' he said to Karen as she slid behind the wheel again. 'Is there a back road?'

'Not a road *per se*, but we can cut across the footy field to get closer to the middle of the town.' She reached for the starter button and let the truck roar to life.

The footy field was empty when they reached it, a wooden fence separating the green stretch of grass from the road. Karen punched through the grey planks leaving gouge marks behind them, cutting the engine when she reached the fence on the other side, which was little more than a pole suspended at waist height.

Luke popped the gun turret open, hoisting himself up so his elbows rested on the roof. He smiled as he looked back down into the truck. 'Now we find the others.'

# Chapter Sixteen

The Melbourne group was suffering for numbers. Their working parties had cleared several of the tunnels and successfully opened up routes to most of the city, but the added freedom had come at the cost of many lives as they stumbled through the dark tunnels. This expansion had brought its own problems as well. Extra eyes were needed to watch over the new entrances for the constant threat of infected, and defend against the new threat of opportunistic hunters that had started to form packs through the tunnels. So far they had been lucky; their first encounter had been reported by a group of their men who had been sent to look for clean water. They had met up with hunters also on their way out to gather supplies.

The scavenging groups had filled the kitchen of the Melbourne hospital and utilised several of the office rooms behind it for extended storage. After the riot over the rationed portions on the first day, a guard had been posted at the entrance to contain any further violence. Several people had died before order had been restored. This had led to Nicholas, a former CEO in the children's hospital, stepping up and organising what people had started referring to as the HYDRA: a sole body of power with many heads in charge of different areas, covering food and foraging, housing, medical care, repairs and communication.

Daniel had been placed in charge of communication, and he was responsible for widening their contact list to include parties in Warragul and Albury to the east, as well as a growing group that had fled to the Grampians. He had also recently made encouraging contact with the HMAS *Canberra*, which had been mobilised and sent from Sydney to the south-east coast of Victoria. They had been taking on passengers at different ports and the Melbourne group hoped to be able to meet up with the ship as it rounded the southern port.

Jen had been kept busy in the hospital bunker as she tried to care for the growing number of injured with fewer and fewer trained staff remaining. The generator fuel had been rationed by the HYDRA, and so they were reduced to primarily using candles picked up during scavenging trips through the day. John Campbell, the orderly who had been bitten by Jen's schizophrenic patient, had turned on the same day as the bite. The homeless woman showed no symptoms; instead she had calmed dramatically. It was a confusing phenomenon. Each of the attack victims who had shown no real signs of turning had actually started to improve to the point of normality. Most now blended in completely with the rest of the group. The homeless woman, who had introduced herself as Peta, now had her hair tied up neatly, revealing a fresh, middle-aged face and Jen had no problems holding a regular, intelligent conversation with her.

In direct contrast, those who had been bitten seemed to undergo a horrific ordeal before turning. Dr Marcus had taken a special interest in John, refusing to allow anyone entrance to the locked room he had been secured in. Jen had heard his cries and moans as the fever wracked his body, which then died off to pitiful whimpers before he sank into silence. Jen had tried to get in at that point, to check on him and give him something to make him comfortable, but Dr Marcus stood firm, not leaving his post by the door. He wrote down all his observations in his little notebooks as the infection progressed, comparing it his information on other infected patients. Peta had been in the room next door for a while until they were sure she wasn't turning. Then she was moved back to the wards under Jen's care and Dr Marcus's scrutiny.

Jen glanced to the corner where the doctor sat hunched over his files, candles throwing their pale yellow light over the pages. He pushed his fists into his eyes and sighed, then threw his chair back and walked toward her.

'I need to see sunlight before I go mad. Do not go in. Do not let anyone else in.'

'He's still alive?' Jen was shocked. They had started euthanising them after they stopped responding to stimulus, so as not to tempt fate by keeping them with the others.

'It,' he emphasised. 'Once they stop responding, it's an "it".' He walked toward the steps that led to the hospital floor above them. Jen pulled his chair out and slid behind the dark desk, picking up the top file and flipping to the handwritten notes at the back.

*1100hrs*

*Patient has succumbed to fever, and no longer responding to speech, light or painful stimuli. HR is still present but extremely bradycardic and thready at 15 bpm. Blood pressure is 30/25, not sustainable to life. Patient has been restrained as precautionary measure. Will continue to observe.*

*1310hrs*

*Patient has shown signs of rousing. HR has persisted in bradycardic rhythm. No change has been noted in other observations. Pupils are fully dilated and non-reactive to light, eyes seem to sluggishly follow the movement of the torch, but has shown no signs of overt aggression.*

*1330hrs*

*Patient has turned, now actively fighting its restraints*

*when I walk through the door, though it remains placid if I am not within eyesight and door is closed. Aggression seems to increase if there is blood present in the room. Have further tested this theory by smearing uninfected blood on a piece of card and sliding under the door. Patient was able to locate the card on the floor and attempted to eat it. May indicate the ability to identify scent, similar to scavenger beasts.*

Jen put the file back on the desk. 'Does that mean they don't actually die?' she mused aloud.

'In a manner of speaking.'

She snapped the folder shut, spinning in the seat to face the doctor. 'I was … I mean … um …'

'It's fine.' He looked at her pointedly until she stood up and moved beyond the curtain.

Jen was uneasy; something about the doctor's demeanour struck her as suspicious.

Dr Marcus slid in to the vacated chair next to the desk and pulled a small red notebook from the lower drawer, opening it to a fresh page and bowing his head to write.

'Patient 12, admitted after sustaining a bite to the thorax. Patient was placed on an automatic obs machine and quarter-hourly stats were recorded as per protocol.'

He pulled a file from the pile on the desk, flipping it open to a printed record of the routine observations taken for every patient admitted. Their pulse rates had slowed to an alarming level and their blood pressure was similar to an officially brain dead person.

'When the patient started to display signs of awareness in spite of these observations, showing signs of heightened aggression, staff were ordered to restrain the patient and put her through an EEG to check for brain activity.'

He flipped to another chart, this one crossed with sharp jerking lines that showed normal brain activity before the patient suffered a seizure, which smoothed into the recognisable flatline of a deceased patient, with only the occasional blip marring the straight line.

'Post seizure, everything except the automatic nervous system was recorded as clinically non-functional. As per findings, the virus appears to replicate enough of the cellular make up to keep some simple bodily functions operational. It maintains a very low energy reading that seems to keep the organs viable at the lowest possible level.' He tapped his pen against the notebook, referring back to the charts in front of him before starting on the next line.

'The host seems to be reduced to absolute basic functions. Readings indicate extremely low pulse, low blood pressure and low respiratory rate, as though those things are almost side effects to semi-functioning organs, instead of a vital function to sustain life. Musculoskeletal function seems to be comparable to that of a toddler, explaining gait and lack of coordination. Current observations indicate the main drive of the infected host is to perpetuate the virus, which is typically done through a single bite. They don't eat for the nutritional gain, but seem to lack the ability to stop feeding once they start.'

Dr Marcus closed the folder containing the charts. He turned to a new page in his notebook and scrawled the word 'anomalies' at the top.

'Some individuals have been observed to show no signs of infection after the bite. Patient assessment seems to indicate that each of these has a diagnosis of schizophrenia. Some studies indicate that regular electrical impulses that allow the brain to identify reality and interact normally with the world around them are absent, or less functional in schizophrenics. My hypothesis is that either the poor communication within the brain, or something unknown about schizophrenia, is stopping the virus from taking over. They still carry the virus, but it's unable to take root and kill off the host.

'The research team in Geelong has not made contact since the explosion that was initiated to hide the first stage experiments. Our methods of transmitting an inert virus into terminal and biologically compromised patients had almost resulted in a breakthrough; one of the subjects undergoing hormone trial 6 seemed to show some signs of intelligence, trying to gain access into a car near the testing area. The initial thought was that he had been able to access dormant memories; however, this theory was unable to be followed through due to the second evacuation.'

Dr Marcus shut the book and slid it back into the bottom draw as one of the communication runners called him to assist with another patient.

Jen slipped past the curtains from where she had been watching, unable to shake the feeling of unease. Slowly she slid the drawer open and retrieved the book that had held the doctor's focus for so long and started to read, growing paler with every neatly written page.

Daniel's runner swept the curtain aside; like other individuals who were confined to their post, Daniel had taken to bribing the older children to act as his messengers within the tunnels.

'Jen, Daniel needs to see you please.' He stood aside to let her pass.

'Right now?' she asked. She and Daniel had grown closer over instant coffees and late night radio surfing, so while the request wasn't surprising, his calling for her when she was rostered on to work was.

The runner shrugged. 'He said it was urgent.'

Jen pushed the chair back and stood, following the young man out the door.

Daniel was talking animatedly into the radio when she joined him in the reception room. He waved her over.

'… can get the party together by the end of the week for sure! Confirm meeting point as station pier?'

'Confirmed,' a no-nonsense voice responded to Daniel's query.

Jen looked at him quizzically and he held up a finger.

'We will radio when we're a day from anchor.'

'Roger that, out.' Daniel replaced the handset and gave Jen the biggest smile she had ever seen.

'What?' she asked. His infectious grin brought a smaller one to her face.

'That was the HMAS *Canberra*. They're rounding Wilsons Prom, so they'll be here in the next few days!'

Jen was still a little confused.

'They have room for us! We can move pretty much our whole group to the ship—it's a floating city!'

'What do you mean "pretty much"?' she asked, her smile slipping a little at leaving any of their group behind.

Daniel winced. 'Well, most of the way is safe … ish, but the last bit will be on the river.'

Jen understood. It wasn't that they wouldn't fit; it was the possibility that not everyone would want to risk the trip, especially if there was no guarantee of survival.

'So we give them a choice then?'

He nodded. 'I spoke to the HYDRA already. They're going to put it out as a suggestion, but some people might think it's safer just to stay here rather than risk their families out there.'

'So a week, huh? Are the tunnels clear to the pier?'

'For the most part. We're clear up to the Yarra, then we'll either have to grab a boat or swim.'

She scowled. 'Swim? In the Yarra? We'd have a better chance at staying alive if we walked through the city naked!'

'So we find a boat and follow the river to the bay and, hopefully, escape.'

Jen felt the stirrings of excitement thrill up her spine for the first time since Boxing Day. They could be safely breathing in fresh air within the week. She slid further back onto the desk so her feet dangled above the floor, nearly dislodging a sheaf of papers. She snatched at the papers but they evaded her grasp, carpeting the floor below. She crouched, still laughing as she pulled the papers into a pile. Her smile faded as she caught sight of what had been written on one of the pages.

'What's this?' she asked, holding the page up to read.

Daniel paled and reached to grab the sheet from her hand. 'Don't read that, Jen. You don't want to know.'

She pinched the paper tightly, looking up at him, eyes glinting angrily. 'What is this?' she asked again slowly.

Daniel sighed. 'The HYDRA wants this kept under wraps. If it gets out, it could devastate everything! Morale is low enough.' He pushed on, not meeting her eyes. 'The plans for explosion? We think it was a sanctioned government faction; they knew what they were doing.' He took in a deep breath. 'It was a military plane, a "spooky". It wasn't sent to wipe out just the "source of the infection".' He crooked his fingers around the phrase. Daniel's voice was low and he kept looking around as though he feared someone would overhear. 'They wanted to destroy the labs at the source of the virus and cover their tracks at the same time.'

'The government started the virus?' she gasped, shocked.

'Lower your voice!' he hissed. 'I have no idea how far this information goes, and the only reason we know this much is because someone overheard their communication with a doctor here.'

Jen thought back to the disturbing find she had made downstairs.

'Here? In the tunnels?'

'We hope not, but our group is the only one we know of that survived locally. From the landmarks and words they used it has to be here. It sounds like they were somehow involved in a treatment study that went wrong. The virus shouldn't have gotten out of the lab, but now that it has, the government is treating it like it's just an extension of their studies.'

'Then why bother burning down Geelong?' Her disgust dripped through her voice and she made no move to hide it.

'Because there is still a majority that disprove of these actions, and in a lawless society, they have no protection. I think they fear that discovery of fault may mean their death.'

'And rightly so!' she snarled, thumping the papers still in her hand onto the desk. She looked down at the floor. 'What if I said I think I might know who they were contacting?'

'What do you mean? You just found this out.'

Jen relayed to him what she had read in the book she had found before she had been called upstairs. Daniel grew agitated as she spoke. When she finished, he took her hand.

'I need you to tell the HYDRA what you just told me. If he is responsible, I don't think it's wise to bring him with us to the ship. But, by the same token, if some decide to stay, he can't be trusted with their wellbeing.' He pulled her to one of the offices they had secured behind the reception. Its window overlooked the car park and, if she wanted to peep through the metal bars that the workers had welded to the window frame, she could see the massing throng that filled the car park, drawn to the few sounds and lights that shone in the dark, silent city.

Daniel sent his runners to gather the heads of the HYDRA, and they sat back and waited.

# Chapter Seventeen

After speaking with her sister, Georgia had not waited on the first day of the outbreak. She and her fiancé Nathan had left soon after she had hung up from the family in Geelong. They only stopped once, donning their uniforms in order to access the base, where they picked up their personal firearms—the only weapons they could gather without raising suspicion—and drove straight out of town. They made good time on the deserted country roads, taking advantage of the state of ignorance that still kept people secure in their homes.

They crossed the state border in the early evening, speeding through Kaniva when it became apparent that stopping there would be a bad idea. The one-road town was already crowded with fully packed cars and campervans that choked any hint of free space. They drove through the Grampians National Park, where they had seen the panicked drivers from the direction of Geelong making their way out of the dying city behind them. She barely spared them a glance, focusing instead on the thought of her own family ahead of her.

They drove through the night, reaching Meredith in the early morning of day two. Georgia had taken over behind the wheel to give Nathan a break, so she was fortunately alert enough to slam on the breaks when she rounded the corner into the small town centre.

Lit up by the washed out headlights was a herd of the bas-tard things, all turning like moths toward the sudden light. The squealing brakes and hard stall of the car woke Nathan with a start. He grabbed wildly at the dashboard in front of him as his fiancé slammed the car into reverse and swung the wheel hard, fishtailing the car furiously. He reached over her and flicked the headlights off, leaving her squinting into the almost dawn light.

'There!' He pointed to a small road, half hidden behind the trees. Leaving rubber on the rough surface, she veered down it and pushed on, low hanging branches scratching along the roof and whipping at the windscreen. The road ended opposite a green expanse and she swung the car to the left. Nathan gestured to a driveway on the left and she pulled in, following the narrow strip to the end. He nodded at the small white church further up the road. 'We'll go in there. I bet it's what your mum will be drawn to. It has a full view of the road coming and going, and there should be a kitchen that takes donated goods for the poor.'

'It's not what I would call secure,' Georgia pointed out, eyeing the open yard that spilled out onto the road.

'We can secure it once we get in. It's still safer than out here,' he reasoned. 'We'll make it safer in the morning.' He climbed out of the car quickly. 'At the risk of sounding unchivalrous, if you can get the bags, I'll find us a way in.' He reached into the glove compartment, pulling out a solid knife and his sidearm, then moved into the bushes.

Georgia looked sceptically at him but pulled out her own gun and walked around to the back of the car, unloading what little they had managed to pack in their mad dash.

Nathan crept back toward her through the low bushes. 'There's a window open in the back and about thirty of the infected in the main hall.'

'Auditorium,' she corrected distractedly. 'I hope you have a genius plan to get them out.'

'Of course! I figured we'd announce a free barbecue out the

front and fling the doors open. That usually brings the masses outside.'

'Oh damn, I forgot the sausages,' she quipped in a deadpan voice.

'No, really, the window is out the back. I think if we get every-thing ready under the window and one of us goes around to open the front doors and make a bit of noise outside, they should go out on their own. The one at the window can then slip in and shut the doors. And there you go, pest-free building.'

'And who is playing pied piper in this scenario?'

Nathan looked a little sheepish. 'That would be you, babe.'

'ME! Why am I bait?'

'The window is just in reach for me and …'

'And I'm short? Is that what you're implying?'

'No … well, yes, actually.'

She scowled at him. 'I'd say you're sleeping on the couch tonight, but that's pretty much a given anyway.' She dumped the bags in his arms, leaving him juggling the awkward package as she stalked to the line of bushes, muttering under her breath. Nathan pulled the bundle into order and chuckled, moving to the back of the white building.

An angry thump from the front of the whitewashed building signalled the doors opening and he slid the window open higher, hefting the bag to his shoulder and balancing it on the ledge. He had seen a narrow bench below the window on his previous check but he didn't want to risk drawing their attention to the back of the church and ruining their plans by dropping the bags. He kept a hand on the top to steady himself as he pulled his body up quietly and turned to sit on the window ledge, swinging his legs around into the single sink kitchen.

There was no movement in the tiny, dark room; the lone door leading out from it looked old but secure, with a window inset halfway up. He slid the bags onto the bench and pulled out his small pistol, moving slowly to the window and peeking through into what looked like a meeting room. Stacked chairs lined the sides between the far wall and a door that looked like it led to the auditorium. He could hear faint growling under the yelling and heavy bangs that he was sure meant Georgia was having fun out the front, and pushed the heavy door open into the meeting room.

He made it as far as the auditorium door before he heard the thumping that was almost drowned out by the noise outside. Behind the chair stacks he saw a faint movement and changed course to investigate. A heavily pregnant woman was scratching at the wall, unable to get to the distraction outside. One of her breasts had been viciously clawed at and flesh and fat hung down the ripped front of her shirt. He stepped back in disgust, not having been this close to an infected person yet. His movement registered enough in the woman's mind that she turned to face the new distraction. Letting out a rough snarl, she lunged toward him, her oversized belly brushing hard against the chair stack beside her and sending it crashing to the floor. He levelled his pistol, firing into her skull twice. She fell instantly and, in the sudden silence, he could hear the snarling outside spilling behind the church. He threw the door open and ran into the auditorium, his pistol held in well-trained hands. Most of the creatures had pushed outside, and he could hear them beating along the sides of the church. Three stragglers had been caught in the maze of pews and he sighted them, squeezing the trigger and felling the first. A brush on his arm had him wheeling to shoot, pulling up abruptly and wrenching the gun to the ceiling when all he saw was Georgia's face.

'The door's still open! I led them round the back, not that I really needed to after you announced your presence.' She grumbled. The creatures still struggling to move through the wooden pews followed their movements as she weaved through the maze to the front door. Nathan shot down the next one.

'I didn't exactly invite the poor thing in for dinner.' He shot the last one as Georgia passed just beyond its reach.

She slipped into the open foyer, which was little more than a reception desk in front of the double doors. A few stragglers had already made their way back to the front and they pawed at the glass that separated them from the noise and movement within. The doors were floor-to-ceiling glass with heavy wood frames that held them in place.

Nathan joined her at the front where she was looking for a way to secure them, pulling the heavy reception desk behind him as he passed it.

'A little help?' he yelled at her.

'You're going to need help if you keep yelling at me like that, mate!' She scowled back but moved to his side to help him push the desk over onto its side, propping the desk top against the door. The desk overlapped on either side of the door, presenting a solid wall between them and obscuring the glass, though it did nothing to dampen the wet thumps and screeching of bone and nails as they ran down the glass outside.

They slumped to the floor, resting their backs against the wall on either side of the desk.

'I need a drink. I really hope they use real wine for the communion here.' Georgia laughed tiredly.

'We'll have a good look tomorrow.'

The benches they chose to sleep on were unforgiving to their backs, and they both felt it when they woke, wincing as they stretched. They spent the next day moving the pews from where they had almost fossilised in place over the decades and built a dam in front of the desk to anchor it in place. They disposed of the bodies of the infected parishioners out the kitchen window.

A secondary entrance had been made above the ancient organ on the altar at the front of the church. It led out onto the roof of the meeting hall and from there the couple threw communion glasses at the cars in front of the church. While the creatures were distracted, Nathan jumped to the ground to scavenge what he could from the houses and the simple general store that serviced the tiny town. When he returned that evening, they fixed a rope ladder to the meeting hall roof and set up what weapons they could gather at different points around the large hall. They fashioned beds from piles of cushions and pillows and covered them with blankets sourced from local residents who no longer needed them. They kept vigil over the road, watching for any signs of survivors who had made it out of town.

Georgia had been on watch when the low rumble of an engine cut through the darkening sky. She was perched on the roof with the Steyr, the only other firearm she had taken with her. She lifted it to her cheek to peer down the scope.

'Nathan,' she whispered, smacking the butt of her rifle on the tiles under her. Two sharp raps was their agreed signal that they had company. He was quick to join her and she thrust the gun at him, pointing down the road. 'Is that Dad driving?'

He lifted the sight and copied her action, smiling. 'Yup, drives better than your mother, that's for sure.'

She plucked a mag torch from her belt and smacked his thigh with it before waving the beam at them. The campervan flashed its high beams once. She knew there was no way her father had recognised her at that distance, but a chance at finding a safe place to rest was worth taking and the campervan turned onto the road that led to the little church, pulling up in front.

Nathan stayed on the roof, scanning their surroundings for any movement while the refugees piled out of the cramped quarters. He could see Alex and Anica step down from the front of the campervan after lifting the bottom of a rough shell of corrugated iron and chicken wire that seemed to surround the vehicle. Alex then slid open the side door. A white-haired man, around the same age as Alex, climbed out next, a bow slung over his shoulder. He turned to help a young girl down, and then another who climbed out holding a bundle to her chest. Nathan could barely make out another shape pressed against the back window but it made no move to exit.

Georgia reached the ground at the bottom of their ladder and ran excitedly around the church, nearly knocking Alex over in her exuberance. She gathered her mother into the embrace, squeezing her parents tightly.

'Georgia? What are you doing here?' her mother exclaimed, returning the desperate embrace as Georgia looked for the rest of her family.

'What … Where's Sarah? And James and Bec?' She looked confused. Alex pulled her in close.

'We had a few hiccups back in town.' Georgia started, pulling back with wide eyes.

'Are they …?' She couldn't bring herself to finish but Alex rushed on.

'No, they're fine, they just had to take a detour. Can we go inside? We can fill you in there, and you can tell me how you happened to meet us here instead of Kaniva.'

'I hate to interrupt,' Nathan called down to them. 'But it seems that the town has sent a welcome committee.' He stood on the edge of the roof, eyes toward the town centre.

'Speaking of welcoming committees,' Georgia looked pointedly at the stranger.

He stuck his hand out. 'Sorry. Joe.'

'Georgia.' She smiled tightly, taking his hand firmly.

'Can I suggest we circle the wagons?' said Joe. 'We passed

enough cars on the way.' He looked up at Nathan and asked, 'How far off are they?'

'Maybe two kilometres?'

'That's plenty. We just need to form a bit of a fence around the front to deter them.'

Joe sorted the group out so half of them pushed the dead cars toward the church. The girls had the job of making sure they lined up in a rough circle around the front, giving them a yard of sorts. By the time they were finished, the group were filthy and tired and collapsed in a heap on the pile of cushions.

Georgia handed out cups of grape juice they had found earlier, and they all drank greedily.

Alex looked thoughtfully into his glass. 'Good year this, nice bouquet.' He nodded decisively and Georgia laughed, curled into Nathan's side.

As the patriarch of the family, Alex volunteered to look out for the rest of his family's arrival. He sat on the roof with Georgia's pistol resting beside him and a riflescope that the new, welcome additions to the group had supplied. As a result he was the first to see them, even though he didn't realise who it was at first. He followed the huge vehicle as it approached, kicking up dust behind it, following its progress as it turned down the rough road leading to the oval, wincing as it snapped fence palings and ripped up grass before it skidded to a halt at the far end. He squinted against the sun, shielding his eyes with a hand before bringing the riflescope to his eye.

The truck's hatch cover flipped up to let a young man in hospital pyjamas lift himself up onto the roof. He was followed by two other men in similar clothes, one clearly the first man's twin, and a young blonde woman. She turned to talk to one of the young men as the twins bent to lift a man through the hatch, taking care not to aggravate an obviously injured leg. Was that Bec? He had almost given her up for lost! The next head to poke through the hatch he recognised immediately.

'James,' Alex gasped, picking up the pistol and tapping the grip sharply against the tiled roof twice, letting out a huge sigh of relief. His kids were safe, his family almost all together once more. He could hear chairs scraping the floor inside the church as they responded to the pre-arranged signal. Anica and Joe opened the door, stepping out into the closed off yard.

Meredith hadn't had a large population to begin with, and the people had apparently been caught unprepared. Creatures still roamed the streets and Alex's group hadn't found any survivors during their escape from Geelong. Now he had to rally them to pick up the last of his family.

# Epilogue

*Melbourne*

The HYDRA had worked quickly, taking Dr Marcus away from the group for questioning. It seemed as though his moral compass had malfunctioned to the point where he felt no remorse or conscience for what had taken place in the name of science. He had been livid at the gall of the 'uneducated civilians' who imagined they could judge him, but having it pointed out that he was in the minority, and presented with the damning evidence in his own hand, he ungracefully relented. He spoke plainly of the progress they had made in the world of virology, referring to the countless unfortunate victims as the tools of advancement. He drew parallels with past prisoner of war experiments and how the test subjects then had been instrumental in modern medicine. In the end the HYDRA council had to restrain one of the members from attacking the doctor. They escorted Dr Marcus out of the room so they could discuss their final decision.

Banishment to the streets was the agreed verdict. Jen was uneasy; she had been included as a witness in case he decided not to cooperate, but thankfully this had proven unnecessary.

She leant over to Daniel. 'That's a death penalty!'

'Would you rather he stayed with the group?'

'Well … no.' She had nothing to refute the argument. He couldn't come with them onto the ship. If he did they would need to put a watch on him at all times with the madness he had been spouting. By the same token, neither could he stay there. Several families had opted to remain under the city, relying on the hard work that had been poured into fortifying the tunnels, rather than taking a chance on a ship that might not be there when they eventually reached the bay.

They drew straws to see who would be responsible for taking the doctor outside. Daniel and a stocky man that Jen had only seen in passing pulled the duty. The group as a whole would walk him up to ensure he was unable to escape, but Daniel and the man had the task of pushing him out the door and closing it again.

They brought the doctor back into the room and informed him of their decision.

'You can't do that.' His face was a dark, furious red, though his eyes betrayed his fear. 'Do you know what I have done? For you! I am the key to the future! I *AM* the future!'

They tuned out his rants as well as they could but Jen saw a number of eyes brushing over him; some with fear, some with fury. None held any compassion.

She had never found herself at the surface door so quickly before, lost as she was in her thoughts. Daniel nodded to a tall, slender redheaded man, who removed the bolts that secured the bed frame across the emergency door. The door opened on to the alley alongside the hospital, which led to the infested street. He pushed the key into the deadbolt and opened the door softly, looking briefly outside. His caution and method marked him as part of the scavenger crew who used this entrance frequently. He stood to the side and Daniel and the other man stepped up with the doctor thrashing between them, still spewing out his vitriol to the group. They threw him roughly out the door and pulled it shut, the deadbolt clicking into place. Daniel walked wordlessly to Jen and pulled her away from the group until they reached the narrow bench he had claimed as his sleep area.

'We killed him, didn't we?' he stated softly. 'We just executed a man.'

'A madman,' she insisted, recognising that it was his turn to be reassured. She pulled on his hand to get him to face her. 'A madman partly responsible for sending this city to hell.'

He shook his head. 'It would have been kinder to slit his throat.'

Jen leaned in close, and wrapped an arm behind him.


The ship called again the next day. Daniel was not on duty at the time, remaining with Jen like a silent shadow while she worked. The HYDRA called a group meeting and the crowd of around three hundred filled the gaps of the hospital foyer where they had gathered. Jeffrey, a soft-spoken man of Asian descent, had been selected as spokesperson.

'As you know by now, we have been in contact with a naval ship off the coast.' There was a murmuring swell in the crowd and many of them nodded. 'An hour ago we received word that they have made anchor a little way out in the bay, and will remain there for the remainder of the day.' The murmur recurred, this time mixed with concern and a little anger.

'A day? Couldn't they have given us a little warning?' A terse voice bounced out of the crowd, the anxious rumblings growing louder. Jeffrey held up his hands for silence but still fought to speak over the noise.

'They have apologised for the short notice. There were some issues onboard, including a problem with fuel, which is why we have such a short time frame to make it there. They need to leave to refuel and we need to be onboard because there is no promise they can return.' The crowd erupted once more but he continued to speak. 'I know that some of you have opted to remain behind in the tunnels and we do not fault that decision, but those of you going to the ship have half an hour to organise your belongings and your families and meet at the Yarra tunnels. We will be leaving in exactly thirty minutes.' He spun on a heel and walked smartly to the stairs that led to the living quarters.

They had been preparing for this eventuality, with a handful of medical staff choosing to stay behind to be with their families. They were prepared to train up others to step into carer roles.

Jen had done her part, making sure the paperwork was all in order for her patients, including the twenty-three mental health patients that they had decided would have to stay behind. There was no guarantee that whatever was managing the schizophrenic symptoms would keep working, and there was no way of managing that many potentially violent patients in such a confined space. She blew out her candle and picked up her small bag, heading for the tunnels where she would meet Daniel.

There were only ninety people in the group who trudged through the tunnels and Jeffrey led them confidently. He was the only person from the HYDRA that had chosen to come, the others staying behind with the group. Jen knew that two had injured family members in the medical wing and a third had a daughter with schizophrenia in the mental health rooms.

Now, everyone looked to Jeffrey. He led them to the mouth of the tunnel where it dropped into a wet drain that spilled into the brown river, and walked along the narrow lip that lined the wall to the jetty where they had secured a dinner cruise boat—the only vessel nearby that would accommodate the group. The lip was low enough that their heads were below street level, but only just. If Jen craned her neck to look skyward, she could see movement along the street and over the bridges that stretched across the river. One of the infected passed close enough to send pebbles raining down on them, making one of the younger ladies further down the line gasp in panic. Those around her shushed her quickly and the feet above moved away.

The boat was large enough to hold them all comfortably and Jeffrey steered it with a practiced hand, taking his passengers out to sea. They passed the once great city as they coasted over the water. Some creatures had noticed their flight and followed them along the shore. The boat kept in the middle of the river, far away from the blackened fingers that reached out for them. As they passed the mouth of the river, the wall of steel that made up the side of the naval ship was clearly seen out in the bay. They eagerly crowded against the side of the small cruise boat that was dwarfed by the larger ship as Jeffrey pulled closer, staring up at the metal colossus in awe as he called them from the radio onboard, alerting them to their approach.

The welcome reassurance came back to them: 'We're lowering the ladder now. We've got you.'

Jen smiled as Daniel hugged her to him.


*Meredith*


The grief was palpable in the small church. James had broken down on Rebecca's shoulder halfway through his retelling. Seth had to step in and relate what little he had seen, gently painting Sarah as a hero who had run to save Nell and had been taken down quickly. Then the explosion that had chased them from the area had stopped them from going back to find her. Rebecca had not let Charlie out of her arms since they walked through the doors, and could only rest her head against her husband's.

Anica had collapsed into Alex, unable to do anything but stare out in front of her. Georgia keenly felt the pain of not seeing her sister again, hiding her face in Nathan's shoulder as the tears came. Seth pulled the others into the meeting room at the back, allowing the family privacy as they grieved together. He knew how they were feeling, having lost his own sister on the first night. Luke and Peter remained close to each other, reliving their own feelings of loss and uncertainty about the safety of the rest of their family. They had been unable to speak to their sister since the railway station and had no idea if she had survived behind the thick walls of the gaol, especially in light of the butchery they had seen at its door.

Seth was lost in half-formed plans. He knew they needed to make a decision to stay or move on. But if they moved on, where would they go? How? Already he could see the rosy glow of unchecked fires from the direction of Geelong, the aftermath of the explosion that had taken the city. He had kept his small group moving, arranging the weapons Georgia and Nathan had brought with them into the secured compartments of the Bushmaster. They kept their limited firearms beside them. Helena pulled the twins aside, directing them to repack the two large cars to share the load and find room for all the supplies they needed to take with them. Cans and dried goods were squirrelled into the cavities and storage spaces, and what little water they had left was split between the two.

Seth felt cruel as he stepped into the spacious room to interrupt the family's thoughts. 'I am sorry, but we need to talk about what happens next. There is a group further down the road behind us that may cause problems, and we need to decide what we do from here.'

Alex looked at him through red eyes. Seth had overheard Rebecca tell them of the biker trouble they had run into, and the threat they posed. Anica pulled herself out of the family gathering. Her face was pale but determined. She called the others in and they filled in the gaps around the family, crowding in close and offering their own silent comfort. Seth remained standing, leaning heavily on his crutches as he brought them all up to speed.

'We have a decision to make. Geelong is gone and there is no going back there. Keep in mind that if we stay, we have a group of … rough people who may come looking for supplies. I vote we don't hang around to offer them a beer. Our other option is to move on.' He looked to Joe. 'You mentioned you were in contact with a group that had headed to the Grampians?'

Joe nodded. 'They said they were headed there, but we haven't heard anything since. We don't know if they made it or not.'

'We drove through there on the way here,' Nathan interjected. 'It may be a safe place to go, but we are by no means the only ones to think of it. On day one alone there were already hundreds of cars on the roads around there.'

'We'll put a pin in it. If there is an established camp there for refugees, it might be a good option. However, if even one infected person got in, that's a lot of people for the virus to get hold of.'

'Sarah wanted us to head north. She said we should go for the Dingo Fence and see if it's enough to keep the bastards out.' James's voice was soft as he spoke.

'How was she planning to get there?' Seth asked.

'Cars where possible, keeping away from the coast and the bigger towns.'

Seth found himself almost missing a person he had never met. Sarah sounded like she would have been a good person to know, cool-headed and organised. It sounded like she was a great loss to the group.

'We've packed the cars up and we'll head out tomorrow.' Once again he looked to Joe, who nodded. They were lucky that the campervan was an automatic so the boys could share the driving. Seth looked at the low hanging moon as the others got comfortable.

Tomorrow they would leave all this behind them; tomorrow, they could start to move on.

## Geelong

Jimmy stood up, his head out the roof of the truck as it bounced over the rubble. The city was burning around them and again he questioned the sanity of this plan. They had moved what was left of their group of survivors after the bombs dropped, thankful that the cold, unwelcoming gaol had been sturdy enough to protect them from both the explosions and the threat of infection.

Aside from one incident, where a party of infected had followed some of their people to the door and needed to be destroyed, there had only been one minor disturbance. The day before, a car had peeled open the fence to the reserve base and another group had driven out in one of the heavy trucks within. The creatures had swarmed into the base after they had left, stopping Jimmy's group from doing the same at the time.

Jimmy had come up with the idea of breaking out over the fence that overlooked the base, and they had dismantled the chain link fences inside the prison, cobbling them together till they were long enough to drape over the razor wire that still topped the prison walls. Eighteen frightened people had crawled up and over, dropping to the roof of the garage. Liberating one of the massive trucks had been simple after that, and they left in the same direction as the last group, watching as the fire consumed the outer suburbs on its slow creep through the city. They had crowded into the truck like sardines, sitting on laps to fit into the twelve-seater truck as Josh drove away.

They crossed the freeway carefully, picking their way over the twisted ruins that merely hinted at cars now. Josh's girlfriend

Megan tapped him on the shoulder, pointing to a blackened sedan that had been thrown hard against the ute beside it by an upturned mini that lay crumpled on its other side. They sped past the few infected residents that still walked along the back roads. They could see three now through the front window, eagerly pawing at the wrecked cars in front of them. Josh made to keep driving, but in the way of girlfriends everywhere, Megan smacked his head and pointed again.

'They only act like that when there's fresh prey to get to. Stop the car now.' Her dark hair hung loose around her face and she tied it back quickly. 'Or I *will* be jumping out of a moving car.'

He shot her a look, clearly questioning her sanity, but pressed on the breaks. Jimmy pulled his head back into the truck.

'She has a point. You keep the truck running. Matt and I will go. You stay.' He pointed a finger at Megan before climbing down the back, Matt at his heels. Jimmy picked up a sledgehammer from the side of the truck. As his weapon of choice, he hadn't let it leave his sight since this whole thing started. Matt carried his crowbar; both had become scarily proficient at wielding them in recent days.

They approached the creatures warily, one eye on the piled up cars around them. The sledgehammer made quick work of the first, crushing bone under its weighty head. Matt hauled out one that had managed to crawl further under the car than the others and buried the pointy end of his crowbar in the base of its skull, severing the spinal cord and destroying the brain from the back. The last body ended a little lower than its chest. Matt grabbed a handful of the shredded shirt and hauled backward, steel meeting skull once more before it, too, fell still. With the growls silenced, they could just make out a soft panting from beneath the rubble.

'Hello?' Matt called, dropping to a knee. A desperate 'Thank God' met them as they worked to pull the heavy metal off the buried woman.

'Look, this is too heavy. Can you move toward us?'

'Yeah, I think so. I missed the worst of it. I guess the car shielded me to a point.'

A shuffling noise preceded the appearance of a grazed, dirty hand that grasped the bumper of the car. A black head of hair followed and the woman struggled to pull herself out. Both boys grabbed hold of a wrist and pulled gently until the filthy woman, dressed in burnt and ripped hospital scrubs, stood before them, badly shaken.

'I'm Matt, he's Jim. Need a ride?' Matt asked, his blinding white smile standing out prominently against dark skin.

'Away from here? Sounds good.' She held out a hand that still shook a little. 'I'm Sarah.'

# THE SOUTH RECLAIMED

IN APRIL 2016

www.facebook.com/TheSouthForsaken

# About the Author

Writing has always been my first passion. I remember swapping spiral notebooks with my friends at high school, each adding a chapter of invented worlds, incredible spaceships, fantastical creatures and imagined rituals. Everything that popped into my twisted head found its outlet through my pen. I don't think it occurred to me that someone else might want to read it.

I can attribute my love of writing to my grandfather. I remember him hunched over his typewriter, pages and pages of poems and memories spilled onto the table around him. I'm not sure how he would have responded to *The South Forsaken*, but I know he would have been proud of another grandchild following in his footsteps.

Follow Rachel on Wordpress:
http://racheldrummond2014.wordpress.com